◄◄◄◄◄◄ WARPED ►►►►►►►

STAR TREK
THE NEXT GENERATION®

◄ ◄ ◄ ◄ ◄ ◄ **WARPED** ► ► ► ► ► ► ►

An Engaging Guide to the Never-Aired 8th Season

Text by Mike McMahan

Illustrations by Jason Ho

Based on the Twitter account @TNG_S8
created by Mike McMahan
and
Based upon Star Trek® and
Star Trek: The Next Generation®
created by Gene Roddenberry

G

GALLERY BOOKS

New York   London   Toronto   Sydney   New Delhi

G

Gallery Books
An Imprint of Simon & Schuster, Inc.
1230 Avenue of the Americas
New York, NY 10020

This book is published by Gallery Books, an imprint of Simon & Schuster, Inc., under exclusive license from CBS Studios Inc.

First Gallery Books trade paperback edition October 2015

GALLERY BOOKS and colophon are registered trademarks of Simon & Schuster, Inc.

For information about special discounts for bulk purchases, please contact Simon & Schuster Special Sales at 1-866-506-1949 or business@simonandschuster.com.

The Simon & Schuster Speakers Bureau can bring authors to your live event. For more information or to book an event, contact the Simon & Schuster Speakers Bureau at 1-866-248-3049 or visit our website at www.simonspeakers.com.

Interior design by Davina Mock-Maniscalco

Manufactured in the United States of America

10   9   8   7   6   5   4   3   2   1

Library of Congress Cataloging-in-Publication Data is available.

ISBN 978-1-4767-7905-8
ISBN 978-1-4767-7906-5 (ebook)

Author's Note

I n the basement of the *Star Trek* archives, behind shelves
of *Enterprise*-D models, bags of wigs, and bins of plastic
phasers, sits a dusty cardboard box with *TNG Season 8*
scrawled on the side in black marker. Inside you'll find a
pile of VHS tapes, labels yellowed with age, that contain
never-before-seen episodes and behind-the-scenes footage
for something truly amazing. . . .

The world thinks there are only seven seasons of *Star
Trek: The Next Generation*, but there's one more.

A *secret* season.

After seven years of sci-fi mysteries, Borg attacks, and
red alerts, the TNG production crew, cast, and writers
had reached their limit. There was little to no downtime
between seasons, and nights were often sacrificed to ensure episodes were delivered on time. The cast was starting
to become one with their costumes, producers were losing touch with reality, and the writers could speak only

in grunts and gurgles. Something had to be done, or the show would destroy their minds.

A secret plan was hatched: they would produce and film a season so un-airable that it would kill the show and allow everyone to finally get a full night's sleep.

At the end of each workday, the entire TNG team said good-bye to their families and dedicated themselves to filming a season as fast as humanly possible. They wrote, shot, and SFX'ed entire episodes in single nights, sustaining themselves on gallons of Jolt cola and cases of microwave popcorn. Complicated sequences were hastily completed in one take, scenery was ripped down and replaced with frightening speed, makeup was practically slapped onto aliens as they ran from set to set. Most of the dialogue was either improvised or called out by writers as they shot each scene; some episodes were really just filmed rehearsals, audio effects provided by the production assistants. Nothing sounds less convincing than a PA yelling "zap zap!" when the *Enterprise* is under attack, but nobody cared: completion trumped perfection.

In the end, due to exhaustion, malnutrition, and twitchy enthusiasm, it was a weird season filled with bizarre choices . . . but dammit, it worked. Paramount couldn't air something so brazenly slapped together and shark-jumpy without killing the franchise, and they needed the TNG cast to remain un-silly for their feature film plans. The show was canceled, and this lost final season was hidden from the world.

The celebration was short-lived, because after a ten-minute catnap, the crew members immediately had to get started on their contractually obligated feature films. But in their hearts, they knew that it could be worse. They had beaten the show, and now they would beat the movies.

I present this very special retrospective so fans everywhere can get a glimpse of the *Star Trek* season that never was (and never should have been). There are rumors floating out in the darkest niches of fandom: some claim Season 8 was accidentally broadcast in Canada for a single weekend marathon, others say there's a way to access the episodes with a specific cheat code hidden as an Easter egg somewhere on the Season 7 DVDs. To this day, there's no confirmed way to watch the final twenty-six episodes. One day, they'll pop up on the Internet, but in the meantime, you'll have to make do with this guide instead.

Each chapter herein starts with a description of the plot, usually broken up into the main story (A-plot), then the secondary story (B-plot). After that, I've transcribed memorable quotes and highlights from the behind-the-scenes material. Due to my tireless efforts, you'll finally be able to complete your knowledge of *Star Trek: The Next Generation*, impressing your friends and infuriating your enemies.

But beware: this season truly goes where no one has gone before. Make sure your mind is up to the task.

I'm being serious here.

I think.

—Mike McMahan / @TNG_S8

◀ ◀ ◀ ◀ ◀ ◀ ◀ **WARPED** ▶ ▶ ▶ ▶ ▶ ▶ ▶

EPISODE 08·001

"Crushers Not Included"

Stardate 47995.8

The *U.S.S. Enterprise*-D zooms through space, narrowly avoiding lots of little rainbow streaks. On the bridge, Counselor Deanna Troi is halfway through a pretty impressive waffle cone sundae when, struck by a massive ice cream headache, she screams, bumps into a console, and rolls on the deck. Revived in sickbay, she describes an intense mint chocolate chip vision: Wesley Crusher and the Traveler both plugged into electronic chambers, surrounded by menacing sugar cones. She's pretty sure the cones and the dancing cherries were constructs of her imagination, but the rest was far too convincing: it had to be real.

The previous year, Wesley forwent his Starfleet career to join the Traveler's exploration of the dimension-verse as a being of pure energy. Wes should be floating around space, examining different cultures, appearing in cloud form doing cloud things (hanging out, observing, drifting)—but Troi thinks her premonition is clear: he's in danger. She tries to convince Captain Jean-Luc Picard that her vision is a creamy cry for help, but they're interrupted by a red alert: the *Enterprise* sensors have detected one of the worst things they can detect—the Borg. Troi is starting to understand what her dream actually meant; she knew those damn sugar cones were up to no good. Now they *have* to rescue Wes. As massive and glorious a vessel as the *Enterprise* is, it still manages to be really good at hiding; the crew tucks her in behind a large asteroid while her sensors peek out to detect dozens of Borg cones swirling around a starship factory. Troi was right, these Borg have upgraded from their usual cubes to the pointier, deadlier, conier shapes swirling before them. Wes and the Traveler must be trapped inside.

Confident that daily yoga and meditation has subdued his Locutus identity, Picard and an away team beam into the factory and find Wesley and the Traveler plugged into the main power relay. The Borg are harvesting their interdimensional energies to power their entire operation; Wes and the Traveler yelp as little diodes zap their heads. Picard climbs up on their enclosure and frees them by pushing down on the lid of their prison and turning it clockwise—back in his Locutus days, he learned the Borg use simple child-safety mechanisms to keep drones from opening containment chambers, getting under the sink, etc.

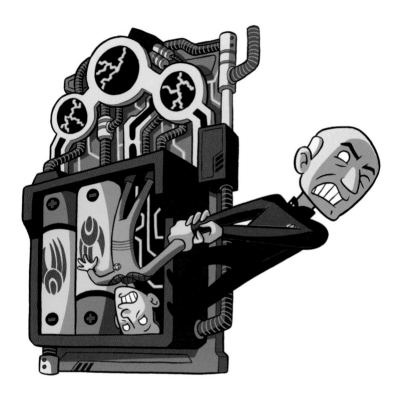

Alerted to their escape, Borg drones now attack in full force. After some wrist chopping and corridor running, they're all surrounded. As they're about to be prodded by the whirring mechanical tidbits on the Borg's hands, the Traveler sacrifices himself, overloading the factory by scattering its matter across an infinity of parallel space dimensions, giving Wes and the captain the time to beam over to the *Enterprise*.

Back in sickbay, Troi offers Picard and Wes sundaes

(she can sense they need to relax, and nothing relaxes like Rocky Road). Picard and Wes are appreciative, but they decide to hook up to medical equipment and get treated anyway because Troi isn't the best authority when it comes to third-degree burns. While the purple lights repair their skin, Picard and Wes discuss the future. The captain consoles his young friend for his loss—he knows Wesley really cared for the Traveler. Wes thanks him, but admits that he's tired of floating around the universe: he misses normal corporeal stuff like eating, cracking knuckles, and waiting in line for things. Even though sticking to one dimension will cause his new powers to quickly fade, he'd like to rejoin the *Enterprise* crew, if they'll have him. Before Picard can speak, he adds that Starfleet Academy can go to hell: he's never going back *there*. Picard welcomes him aboard the ship and appoints him the rank of honorary cadet. Wes is slightly miffed, thinking he should probably have a higher rank, on account of hello, all the godlike knowledge he's been gathering? But this request is greeted with a hearty laugh from Picard, Dr. Crusher, the assistants in sickbay, and some ensigns who happened to be passing by.

The secondary storyline features a more personal adventure. Left in charge of the *Enterprise* while Picard is leading the rescue team, Commander William T. Riker is trying to concentrate on his duties, but he's having a hard time because he's distracted by his new, high-tech sleeping blouse. The LuxComfort Ultra Blouse is composed of nanotech memory silk that can read and remember how each of his romantic partners prefers the garment to hang off his body (some of the ladies like to see that upper thigh hair, while others prefer to leave that to their imaginations). The blouse changes color depending on the level of flirtation Riker's throwing down, and his initials are microscopically embroidered on both breasts, the lapel, and all over the back. But during the Borg confrontation, it's just common sense to have all power diverted to the shields, just in case the Borg get too frisky . . . and without an energy source, the LuxComfort blouse starts glitching out. It constricts, rolling Riker up like an elegant silk burrito. Then, it grows

so large he can hardly move, swimming in a sea of shimmering blue fabric. Riker has always been adept at fighting his way out of things, and this garment is no different. He uses some rarely utilized textile jujitsu to free himself, but the blouse isn't going to fold. It goes after Troi, dragging her away from Riker faster than he can full-sprint after it.

Once the Borg have been defeated, the *Enterprise*'s power is restored, and Riker is able to rescue Troi, who has been dangerously draped in the blouse's deadly trim. Riker tames the blouse with a molecular hanger, safely sheathing it in a garment bag. Struck down by his own hubris, Riker is now aware of the dangers of such a high-tech frock. He locks it away and goes back to his trusty, old-fashioned nightshirt. However, the LuxComfort doesn't like being locked away in a dark closet with Halloween costumes and out-of-style winter coats. It is patient garb, and one day it will have its revenge . . . unless it gets thrown out or donated.

Memorable Quotes

TROI

They were plugged into some kind
of machine, being tortured. It was
horrible.

RIKER

Touch my blouse. It'll relax you.

TROI
(shaken, ignoring him)
I'm serious, Will. It seemed so
real.

RIKER
Shh. It's blouse time.

WESLEY
Captain, I knew you'd come!

PICARD
(whispering)
Quiet, Wesley. Our safety depends
on our discretion. We have to be
vigilant not to alert the Borg to
our—

WESLEY
(screaming)
*I can't wait to get back to the
ship and see my mom!*

Intruder alarms start blaring.

Trivia

✦ Viewers might recognize the Borg wall alcove Wesley is trapped in. It's actually a tanning bed, spray-painted black with rubber hoses attached. The Season 8 writers demanded it be built into the episode because it looked so futuristic, but mostly so they could have a tanning bed. From this episode on, most pictures of the crew feature them with bronzed, golden skin.

+ Camera operators had to be very careful during the filming of this episode, as the props department was out of dummy prop phasers and had to use real ones. Dangerous and unpredictable, real phasers are usually wielded only in close-up shots because of the high insurance premiums required (premiums that rose dramatically after an extra was disintegrated during the filming of the TOS episode "Friday's Child").

+ The silk for Riker's sleeping blouse exhausted the entire annual silk budget for both Paramount's film and television studios.

Mistakes and Goofs

+ The first Borg drone that the *Enterprise* away team encounters should not have waved or said "Um, hey." A Borg drone would never do this, and, even if so, would only have been on *Star Trek: Voyager*. Eagle-eared viewers can also hear the same Borg say "I think Claire's leaving me" later in the episode.

- This is the only episode where Wesley Crusher has a spider face-tattoo. It was ultimately removed for later episodes because aggressive arachnid face art didn't fit his character, even if it did make him look cool.

- An erotic dance sequence with the silk sleeping blouse was cut from the final edit, making Riker's sweaty Bob Fosse–entrance to the bridge seem out of place.

When Riker needs a shirt to be smooth yet billowing, a blouse is the way to go. Pictured here, the LuxComfort blouse prepares to drape its victim in pain.

EPISODE 08·002

"Lecture Circuits"

Stardate 47999.5

The *Enterprise* is docked in Earth's orbit so it can be refitted with new system programming, upgraded weapons, and probably a couple new holodeck errors. Data takes the opportunity to visit Starfleet Academy to give a lecture on "How to Make Best Friends on Long Voyages." Things take a dark turn when he notices some of the cadets seem to dislike him. (Data isn't the best at reading emotions, so at first he thinks they're hungry.) He finds hateful, anti-android graffiti spray-painted on his car (BATTERY SUCKER), and someone keeps leaving flaming bags of magnets on his front stoop. Data's beloved, elderly neuropsych professor, Dr. Christoph Westlake, suggests he leave campus before some idiot student goes too far, but Data decides it would be safer for androids everywhere if he addressed the problem head-on. He arranges for a symposium on non-carbon-based life and invites famous tripolymer entities to speak out against synthetic bigotry. A bunch of notable silicon rights activists show up, including:

+ **HARGON**—An Andorian war construct with giant sword arms and a nuclear bomb for a heart. Hargon is now a champion of non-violent protest, and uses his deadly sword arms only for educational purposes.

+ **RAD**—He raps, he educates, he downloads the memories of entire civilizations and seeks to understand human emotions. Rad is the embodiment of '90s street knowledge, with righteous 'tude and a borosilicate outer shell that can withstand pressures up to sixteen thousand pounds per square inch.

+ **EXOCOMP 77**—Formerly a repair unit (the exocomps gained sentience back on Stardate 46316.6), Exocomp 77 is a popular romance novelist and knitting enthusiast. His/her most popular novels, *Two's Company*, *Three's a Crowd*, *π Is the Ratio of a Circle's Circumference to Its Diameter*, and *Your Mother Hates Me*, have sold more than seventy billion copies across the Alpha Quadrant.

+ **PLIMP**—An angry, thunderous, metallic ball that constantly discharges plumes of blue fire in every direction. Plimp spends weekends as a volunteer, teaching literacy skills to orphans, who grow accustomed to his flames.

+ **EBRA**—Half zebra, half computational inorganism, this mech-zebra cop fights anti-robot crime and poachers on the metallic plains of Serengeti 5, the android/animal refuge planet.

+ **HOVER CAR**—Celebrity dancer, formerly a family's hover car.

In the Blood Worm Awareness Conference Hall, Data takes the podium in front of half the academy members, who have gathered to hear him speak. Halfway through introducing his guests, Data interrupts himself by jumping off the stage and throwing a particularly burly student out of his chair, revealing a bomb under his seat. He disarms the bomb in front of the student body, resulting in a standing ovation.

Dr. Westlake congratulates Data and tells the crowd they should never forget they were saved by an android that was more human than any bigot. Data isn't buying it; he recognized the bomb's anti-positronic gurminium alloy that only Dr. Westlake has access to. Westlake sneers and admits that he secretly despises androids because they don't age or get progressively more ugly like he does. Westlake's got degenerative facial asymmetry disorder, a disease of the skull that makes his face slightly creepier year after year, and it's driven him mad. Androids don't have to deal with lopsided faces, and he hates them for it. The blast would have taken out every smug synthetic loudmouth in the system. Data tells Westlake there's a place he can live without having to be near artificial life forms: the slammer. He hands him over to campus security, then throws the biggest, coolest party Starfleet Academy has ever seen, where he wins three dance-offs and makes out with a sub commander named Linda. Future Starfleet cadets pass down the legend of Data's party, which went on for more than seventy-two hours and was rumored to have included a drinking game re-creation of the Khitomer Massacre, an epic telling of *The Iliad*, and at one point Data jumping out of the pool and up onto the roof of a building, which nobody had ever done before.

Meanwhile, unaware of Data's academic adventures, Captain Picard and Commander Riker are using the ship's downtime for a camping trip on Runyan 8, a popular great outdoors M-class planet. Everything goes great (Picard shows off his various bird calls and whistling skills, while

Riker karate chops a twig so hard it catches fire) until a five-legged alien bear wanders onto their campground, eats all of Picard's precious heirloom rhubarb, then sticks around to attack them. Riker tosses Picard into a tree, then stands his ground and fistfights the giant ursan, relying heavily on "the Riker Maneuver" (punching with both fists at once while kicking with both legs at once). Muscles stretch to their extremes, sweat flies, knuckles hit fur, paw strikes muscle. Riker and the bear are evenly matched.

Picard shakes the tree's branches and yells encouragement to his Number One, but he stops when the tree asks him to knock it off. Picard has seen some pretty crazy stuff in his day (like the time his replicator made a green

potato chip), so a talking plant doesn't faze him. He strikes up a conversation with the chatty birch and learns that everything on this planet is connected, like a grand global web of information. The tree assumes humans share a similar connection and refuses to believe Picard's claims that they're individuals. Picard has seen this kind of thinking with the Borg, and he knows that no amount of explaining is going to sway this thing's branches—he'll have to prove it. He convinces Riker to let the bear get the advantage. As soon as Riker stops his whirlwind attack, the creature sends him flying into a mud pit, where it pins him, scrabbles at his back, and gnaws on his head. Riker doesn't know what the captain is planning, but he hopes it works soon, because he hates it when his head gets gnawed on. When the tree sees that Riker's injuries don't transfer to Picard, it's convinced that they're indeed individuals, which it describes as "icky." Since everything on this planet shares a consciousness, the bear stops attacking Riker and wanders away while Picard is delicately dropped to the ground like a used tissue. The tree demands they leave the planet, now, and to not touch anything on the way out (it doesn't want any of their gross free will to rub off on anything). Picard thinks the tree is being kind of harsh, and he tries to explain that aliens can work together to rise above their differences, but the tree loudly hums a song to drown him out and throws purple alien pinecones at them until they beam out.

Trivia

+ Bigotry against Data is a recurring theme in *Star Trek: The Next Generation*, but this is the first episode where Data physically throws a bigot. In the twenty-fourth century, throwing someone isn't as dangerous as we view it today, as medical advances have neutralized any physical harm. That being said, to throw someone who isn't prepared is akin to high-fiving a stranger, which can be confusing and rude.

+ The alien bear that attacks Riker was played by Rocko, a noted stage donkey renowned for his ability to "bear it up."

Mistakes and Goofs

+ When Data tours the Starfleet Academy campus, he remarks that the petunias are looking lovely. Viewers will have no problem seeing that the object being discussed is, in fact, a large rock with a sticky note on it. The note reads, "Daryl, please replace with SFX flowers in post." Since no record of a Daryl exists on the Season 8 crew, one can only wonder which Daryl they thought would take care of it.

✦ When Picard yells, "Watch out for the shark!" the actual line read, "Watch out for the bear!" Actors often improvise lines they feel will work better for their characters; other times, though, they think a shark would be way cooler, and are trying to force the special effects guys into altering the design of a space bear.

✦ Large sections of Starfleet Academy are very obviously matte paintings, especially evident since sharp-eyed viewers can see the artist's signature in the lower right-hand corner. If one pays close attention at the eleven-minute mark, Data and his professor can be seen walking through the painted glass, shattering it into a billion pieces. Being consummate professionals, they play it off like it's no big deal, brush the shards out of their hair, and continue on without appearing to be in lacerated agony.

The famous photo of Exocomp 77 passionately advocating
robotic rights at the Vulcan Freedom Festival.

EPISODE 08-003

"Suggested Donation of Danger"

Stardate 48015.1

The *Enterprise* has been docked at Marmullian Zacow, a swanky space hotel, for more than three hours while Geordi and Data dispute damage charges on their bill that claim they flooded a room trying to make a water slide. (They did.) Swayed by a pamphlet he finds in the hotel lobby, Captain Picard decides their next destination is Brodo-5, the Museum Planet.

Brodo-5 boasts more than fifty million museums, and its inhabitants adhere to a strict class system: the wealthy ruling curators revile the underclass docents. There is no aspect of life here that doesn't take place in or act in service of its various institutions. Originally created and colonized by the other four Brodo planets as a place to cooperatively store and display art, artifacts, and scientific discoveries of the combined heritages of the entire system, it is now mostly used as a place to take the kids on weekends. In its heyday, Brodo-5 was the most popular recreational world in the sector; now the planet is outshined by the much more popular Brodo-6, which boasts miniature golf and where juveniles eat free after the binary solstice.

The away team's plan to meet for lunch at Equatorial Food Court Island is thrown into disarray when quiet but knowledgeable docent separatists abduct Commander Riker to display him in their Hall of Amazing Men. Picard seeks intervention from the curators, who refuse to get involved, leaving him with no other option: they'll have to break into the museum and steal Riker back.

In the Hall of Amazing Men, Riker finds that the other humanoids on display are pretty badass dudes. He quickly asserts his dominance by bench-pressing the alpha-male and then lays out his escape plan. The other specimens concur with his scheme, but before they escape, they want to have a bench-press competition. Riker agrees.

Guided by an audio tour and a foldout map, Picard (dressed in all black clothing and a black skull cap), Data (disguised as a statue), and Geordi (disguised as a shrub with a VISOR) overcome a series of security measures and booby traps to break into the museum.

Once inside, they're surprised to find that Riker and the other sensational beings on display have already freed themselves from their exhibits and are nowhere to be found. As they investigate the empty dioramas, the alarms activate, and within moments, the pursed-lipped docents have Picard and his team surrounded.

As the docents prepare to archive Picard on a high shelf way in the back of the basement, Riker and the phenomenal living exhibits stage a counterattack. After some virtuoso hand grappling and backflips, Riker's museum men drive the docents out into the Realistic Forest of fiberglass trees and plastic moss. Soon the away team is safely back in the Museum of Museum Studies at the University of Museum in New Museum, the capital of Museumtucky. Next time, Picard won't be so easily tempted by a pamphlet he finds in a three-star hotel.

While Picard and Riker are occupied with their dangerous field trip, Worf is in the *Enterprise* sickbay after intentionally triggering his vicious peanut allergy. Dr. Beverly Crusher administers yet another epinephrine hypospray and admonishes him for being too cavalier with his snacks; he knows nuts close his airway, inflame his brow ridges, and blind him. Worf doesn't care: allergies are dishonorable and he's going to do whatever he wants. In an act of defiance, he tries to eat a peanut in front of Dr. Crusher, but she slaps it out of his hand.

It's Tuesday, which is when Worf visits the holodeck to fight his internal demons in hand-to-hand combat. He summons a holographic factory that produces candy bars and also processes nuts. Burly demons with skinless skulls come at him with bow-staffs and laser whips. He tries to keep focus as the nutty air chokes him and swells his eyes shut, but the demons gain the upper hand. They pin him to a pile of garbage and rub candy bars in his hair. Luckily, the safety protocols kick in before Worf suffers permanent legume damage.

Back in his quarters, Worf receives a video call from the Klingon High Council; the members think it's hilarious and shameful that he's been undone by tasty treats. He demands to know how the council always has inside info on his shortcomings. They mock him instead—they don't have to dig deep when Worf constantly broadcasts his complaints and weaknesses to anyone who will listen. Eager to prove he's not afraid of a confectionary death, Worf chops a jar of peanut butter in half and proceeds to shovel it into his mouth with the scoop of his *bat'leth*, in accordance with the teachings of Kahless. (Kahless was known to consume nut butters over the graves of his enemies before he would dance the night away, oftentimes waking up the next morning surrounded by his enemies' friends and family trying to hold a memorial service.)

Worf's tendency to ignore health advice is something Dr. Crusher is well aware of, which is why she's implanted a sensor in his thigh that detects when his body goes into a state of shock. The ship computer alerts her to Worf's condition, and she finds him lying on the ground, convulsing and still making "yum" noises. She tries to save his life, but he continues to cram peanuts into his mouth. Not one to be stymied by a challenge, Beverly hooks Worf up to an untested and dangerous Klingon medical device that simultaneously heals while physically punishing the patient. Against the odds, Beverly saves Worf, curing his allergy by grafting peanut RNA onto his cellular index. Worf roars in victory and treats himself to a replicated bag of jumbo shrimp, unaware that a new allergy will soon rear its delicious head.

Memorable Quotes

PICARD
Tell me, is there any part of the planet that isn't a museum?

LEAD CURATOR
Sure, there's the Great Barrier Coat Room, the Icy Parking Lots of the North, and the wonderful Gift Shop Island.

GEORDI
Gift Shop Island?

PICARD
(*sighing*)
Maybe on the way out.

GEORDI AND DATA
YAY!

Geordi and Data perform their signature high five, a choreographed routine that takes up to three minutes to complete.

Riker addresses the males on display.

RIKER

So we're in agreement. After we
escape: push-up contest. The winner
gets to choose what we do next—
lumberjack stuff or fight fires.

STRONGEST BRIAN

What if it's a tie?

RIKER

Hell, that's not unlikely. If it's
a tie . . . we just go eat raw
meat. *All of us.*

The men growl their agreement.

WORF

(*addressing a peanut*)
You expect me to crawl on my belly,
like a kagH? I've killed men far
crunchier for less.

*Worf shakes the peanut, then makes it speak
in a high-pitched voice.*

PEANUT

Eat me, coward.

CRUSHER

Prepare the restraint beam.
I need twenty milligrams of
neuroinhibitor, and get that damn
cookie out of his mouth.

WORF

(*mouth full of cookie*)
Someone got cookie in my peanut
butter!

CRUSHER

That was you, Worf. Nobody's
touching your peanut butter but you.

WORF

MORE COOKIES.

*Nurse Ogawa reaches for the cookie jar, and
Beverly grabs her.*

CRUSHER

Don't listen to him!

Trivia

+ The talking wooden dinosaur skeleton that Geordi
  befriends on Gift Shop Island was originally written
  to return with the away team as a potential new ad-
  dition to the *Enterprise* crew, but budget limitations
  forced the writers to abandon the plan. They later

brought the character back, with slight modifications, as Ensign Harry Kim in *Star Trek: Voyager*.

✦ The explosion effect in the Fireworks Museum was created by holding a candle up to a prism and just shaking it.

Mistakes and Goofs

✦ In his dream when Worf fights the giant jar of peanut butter with a glowing fork, the Klingon flag should not be at half-mast in the background, and the peanut butter should be smooth (as indicated by the label), *not* crunchy. These mistakes ruin potentially what should have been a poignant and emotional fight sequence.

Other Snacks That Have Bested Worf

✦ Hot Juice (mouth burned)

✦ Carrot Dippers (extreme dislike at the thought of eating something orange)

✦ Chip Crumbs (beard ruined)

✦ Bowl of Ice and Hot Sauce (honorable, but too cold and spicy)

✦ Hash (angered by concept)

Some Amazing Men from the Hall of Amazing Men

- **Sweet Conrad**—friendly pirate who fights with poison-laced swords.

- **Strongest Brian**—can do wheelies in any vehicle; a single, thick chest hair dangles off his torso like a rope.

- **Brave Steven**—accomplished chef; knows all knots.

- **Big Shakespeare**—playwright; can crush a man with bare hands.

- **Gregory St. Beard II**—builds pleasure yachts from scratch; has a time-traveling gun.

- **Qorpo w'Ark**—invented reverse punching and the three-hour kick.

- **Gary Mitchell**—still alive, still causing trouble.

- **Zizz the Destroyer**—destroys, educates.

- **Tuk the Destroyer (no relation to Zizz)**—doesn't destroy things; can shoot lava from his mouth, but usually refrains.

Worf's been naughty.

EPISODE 08·004

"Hair of the Synthadog"

Stardate 48017.3

Dr. Beverly Crusher and Counselor Deanna Troi are wrapping up their final day of a Starfleet medical conference on fabulous Jessica 8 (the eighth moon in the Jessica system). Beverly is excited to get back to the *Enterprise*; she has her fingers crossed some incurable disease pops up so she can show off some of the neat experimental procedures she's learned in the last couple days. Deanna is also happy that the conference is almost over, because it'll mean the end of Dr. David Krrgvanimanpon's attempts at trying to impress her. The Pigmalinite doctor's nonstop flirtations, love letters, and physical stunts grew tiresome in less than an hour. If Troi had to spend one more day watching him try to do a backflip, she'd go crazy. Unfortunately, they'll have to endure the conference a little longer, because as the final speech is coming to a close, the lights shut off and the conference hall is attacked by the dreaded Broheims. The Broheims are a Jessica-system pirate clan dedicated to pilfering, destroying, and partying. Beverly has treated Broheim victims in the past—she knows they torture people by forcing them to dance until dead, as well as play Spin the Bottle of Punching and increasingly intoxicating drinking games. As Girtroy, the five-armed pirate leader, concentrates on robbing the other scientists of their jewelry, reading glasses, and Erlenmeyer flasks, Beverly mixes up a hypospray and injects herself. Girtroy yells at her to stop non-partying and tosses her hypospray into his bag, along with her and Troi's combadges and a bottle of positronic brain cleaner that Data asked them to pick up. Troi is bummed: Data was really excited for that cleaner.

Unable to contact the *Enterprise*, Beverly and Deanna can only watch as their fellow convention attendees are forced to participate in various party games, each succumbing to overwhelming intoxication as they are unable to flip cups, accurately bounce metallic currency into pint glasses, or when they're trapped by an ancient restraint called "Edward 40 Hands." Troi can sense they're in over their heads, but as Girtroy approaches them with cups and Ping-Pong balls, Beverly stands up and challenges him to compete at his own games. Deanna is shocked. Beverly can't take this guy on—he drinks for a living! Not only is his alcohol tolerance through the roof, who knows if it even affects his alien physiology? Beverly tells her not to worry: she calls Girtroy a jerk and questions his commitment to drinking. Girtroy can't ignore being called a jerk in front of his crew, especially not from a lowly human who has far fewer arms than a proper species should. He sets up an elaborate tri-level beer-pong court—they'll see who the jerk is.

To Troi's dismay, Beverly is terrible at tri-level beer-pong. Every time she misses a shot, Girtroy lands a ball in one of her cups, forcing her to drink the contents: room-temperature Vulcan ale. Soon, Dr. Crusher has consumed twenty-seven glasses of the foamy brew. Deanna is shocked when Beverly shakes it off and challenges Girtroy to a second game: an old-fashioned drink-off. The alien pirate is surprised, too: he's never seen someone consume

that much Vulcan ale, or that many Ping-Pong balls, and still be on her feet. He accepts.

Troi manages to get a moment alone with Beverly as the pirates set up the next event. Dr. Crusher admits that she injected herself with an anti-intoxicant: she can drink as much as she wants, and it won't have any effect. Troi is worried that makes her a cheater, and sullies the good name of the Federation, but Beverly tells her to take a chill pill—she's just doing what's needed to get them out of a tricky situation. Troi crosses her arms: she will *not* take a chill pill. Cheating is not cool, even under the most perilous of circumstances. Beverly can't believe she's being high-roaded when she's actively saving everyone in the room. Troi relents: they can argue Federation ethics when they're safely back on the ship. Beverly rolls her eyes: like Picard doesn't break the Prime Directive every other week.

Beverly and Girtroy sit across from each other at a table that's completely covered in fancy mixed drinks. Whoever keeps their composure the longest wins. They both start tossing back Regulan Shuttle Bombs. Regulan Shuttle Bombs are not a drink to mess around with: they can literally rewrite your DNA if you aren't careful. Five glasses in, both Beverly and Girtroy are doing fine. Girtroy is confident there's no way she can outdrink him. He was born in an abandoned brewery; he grew up eating hops and fermented Grabarian potatoes. Beverly rolls up her blue sleeves: is he going to talk, or get down to business? Girtroy redoubles his efforts: it is *on*.

Sixteen glasses in, Girtroy tries to stand up, manages to belch out a halfhearted comment about potatoes, then passes out in front of his crew. This is particularly bad for his species because blacking out activates the dance and fart centers of their brains. Troi tosses Crusher a combadge and signals for the *Enterprise* to come kick Broheim butt as Girtroy unconsciously toots and flails across the room. A squad of security teams beam in and swiftly take down the pirates, who aren't so tough when they aren't forcing people to Edward 40 Hands. Dr. Crusher and Troi return to the *Enterprise*, give Data his brain cleaner, and impress everyone in Ten-Forward with Crusher's knowledge of some pretty great new bar games. Then they spend the night arguing about Federation ethics as Guinan tries to tune them out. There is literally no conversation held more often in Ten-Forward than Federation ethics violations. You'd think people would talk more about science, the human condition, their place in the universe, theology: but no. Ethics. Hoo-boy. Guinan keeps her comments to herself and sneaks a little nap while they have at it.

During Crusher and Troi's trouble with tipple, Geordi discovers that someone left a sandwich inside the warp core assembly, and now it's full of orange Mzzk ants. (Mzzk is a particularly pleasant planet to picnic on, but is host to some of the peskiest insects in the sector.) The alien bugs have chewed through connections and burned out a ton of relays, plus they emit an unpleasant odor that makes them practically unapproachable. Or maybe that's just the sandwich. Geordi and Data get to work cleaning the Mzzk ants out of the core, unaware that one of them—the resplendent queen—has crawled into the dilithium chamber to gnaw on the crystal. A sinister music cue plays over her munching noises as her mandibles clack and spark.

A Romulan patrol ship de-cloaks off the bow and demands to board the *Enterprise* just as Geordi cleans out the last of the ants. The Romulans refuse Captain Jean-Luc Picard's attempts to amicably part ways and proceed to steeple their fingers and power up their weapons. At the same time, Geordi and Data find that the resplendent Mzzk queen has grown to an enormous size—a cellular expansion activated by exposure to dilithium radiation and the nutritional properties of the sandwich. She takes hold of an unlucky ensign and shakes him furiously, just out of Data's reach. Data tries to knock him out of her grasp with a Starfleet standard-issue broom handle, but she's too evasive. The queen then proceeds to rampage through engineering, pumping out giant orange Mzzk eggs on exposed electronics, shorting out the *Enterprise*'s shields.

The Romulan captain chortles as he commands his boarding party to take the ship—they'll dispose of the crew, harvest the computer for juicy Federation secrets, then blow it up to conceal the dead. Playing it cool, Picard pretends to worry about their impending attack as

he taps a discreet command into his chair's terminal. Just as the giant Mzzk queen is about to snap the ensign in half, she and her eggs are beamed out of engineering and appear on the bridge of the Romulan ship. A confused moment of silence passes, then the Romulans shriek as the queen starts attacking them and dumping eggs. Picard has utilized his favorite battle tactic: the Tribble Maneuver. When a Starfleet ship is overrun with an invasive species, the captain is authorized to beam it aboard enemy vessels. While all forms of life are owed respect, the Federation makes allowances for certain situations, because seeing your enemy's shocked expression as they face unexpected natural forces is too good to pass up. The *Enterprise* continues on its way as the Romulan ship starts to spin in place, its captain pinned under a hairy thorax.

Memorable Quotes

Dr. Crusher successfully lands a Ping-Pong ball in Girtroy's cup.

> **DR. CRUSHER**
> (*victoriously*)
> There are ten lights!

> **GIRTROY**
> What does that even mean?

> **DR. CRUSHER**
> It's an *Enterprise* in-joke. You
> wouldn't understand.

> **GIRTROY**
> Whatever. We have in-jokes, too.
> Isn't that right, guys?

His men don't know what to say—they don't have any in-jokes.

> **GIRTROY**
> (*grouchy*)
> Just play the damn game.

DATA

It appears that the warp core has a case of ants in the pants, does it not?

GEORDI

Oh, Data.

DATA

I have one hundred and fifty-seven thousand additional ant jokes. Perhaps one of those would be to your liking?

GEORDI

No.

DATA

Perhaps you would prefer jokes about uncles, instead of ants?

GEORDI

I'd prefer to flip that little piece of your scalp up and turn you off, how about that?

DATA

I would like to see you try.

Troi watches Crusher and Girtroy as they have their drink-off.

TROI

I sense an overwhelming
emotion . . . I sense that
Girtroy . . . is a *jerk*!

The pirates gasp.

CRUSHER

Oh snap!

GIRTROY

Real nice. I thought you were
doctors.

The ladies mockingly dance at his expense.

GIRTROY

Wow.

DATA
(*flailing*)
I am covered in ants. Geordi, *I am covered in ants*.

GEORDI
(*slapping at him*)
Hold still, hold still!

DATA

If they get inside of me, you must
promise that you will burn me.

GEORDI

We aren't letting that happen,
Data. Not again.

Trivia

✦ This isn't the first time Dr. Beverly Crusher has fought intoxication. In the rarely seen newspaper-syndicated comic strip *Star Trek: The Next Generation Funnies*, Crusher saves Picard by drinking an entire tequila panther as it lunges at the captain. In the world of *TNG Funnies*, panthers made of tequila are a reoccurring antagonist, just one of many elements that are not considered part of the *Star Trek* canon. Other non-canon elements: Picard's talking cane, Riker growing an extra eye, Wesley's helicopter backpack, and Worf's constant breaking of the fourth wall (which was often employed to advertise trading cards and cereal to the young readership).

✦ Troi's seductive fifteen-minute dance sequence to distract the Broheim guards was chosen by the producers as their favorite guard confusion dance sequence in *Star Trek*'s run. Broken into two parts, this is the only seductive *Star Trek* dance sequence to continue across a commercial break.

✦ Only one ant was harmed during the filming of this episode, and that was because a tiny ant hawk flew onto the set, swooped down, and carried it off. An expensive anti–ant hawk turret was installed, and the rest of the episode was filmed without incident.

Less-Popular TNG Era Cocktails

Regulan Shuttle Bomb

Drop a shot glass of Armus into a Romulan ale, then crack an egg of solidified tequila into the brew. Lick *gerg* off your wrist, down the drink, then bite a Ceti eel.

Qo'noS CoolatA

Dirt beer, blood, and lime. Best served in a glass carved from the skull of a slain enemy, or a regular glass that you've used as a weapon.

Cardassian Spy

Scotch, synthescotch, holo scotch, and a cherry. Drink furtively.

Pulaski's Drink

Brandy with a whisper of skim milk floated on top.

Eugenic War

A piece of felt, soaked in rye whisky overnight, set on fire, and eaten like a steak with a knife and fork.

Flaxian Flu

A mixture of white and dark Flaxian rums. Consumed by having your bartender dip an arrowhead, the tip of a sword, or a dart in the drink, then allowing him to hunt you around the parking lot, injecting a tiny bit of the beverage with every attack.

Warp Core Breach

Frozen beer with a red-hot lava rock beamed into the center.

Risky Maneuver

Three shots of Yorian vodka, dumped on a table, consumed by slurping it up before it spills off the edge and onto the floor. No hands!

Paradise Snare

Kor ale with pineapple DNA microscopically laced around the rim of the glass.

Yesterday's Tomorrow Today

Only available during time quakes, reversals, and rifts. The drinker must reach through a temporal distortion and grab whatever bottle of liquor that exists tomorrow and drink it today, often garnished with a butterfly wing.

The Grouchy Bynar

A series of shots of any type of brown liquor, where each pair of shots has a ratio that's the same as the ratio of their sum to the larger of the two shots in the series.

Buffer Buster

Take any drink, put it through the transporter, and pull the plug while it's halfway phased back. Drink before it causes a singularity. Usually served with a last will and testament loaded up on a padd; before drinking, you have to sign off with a thumbprint.

Neural parasites attach themselves to a host's spine and take control of the brain for years. They also taste great in a martini.

EPISODE 08·005

"I Only Have Mitochondria for You"

Stardate 48022.3

Dr. Beverly Crusher angrily cracks a test tube in half and throws it in the trash—it lands on a pile of similarly broken test tubes. She's at the end of her rope: an alien virus has spread to more than half the *Enterprise* crew, and she has no clue how to cure it. The ship has seen better days: most of the crew is quarantined in their quarters, leaving it understaffed. A lonely tumbleweed made of carpet fiber and hair rolls down an empty hallway. It bonks into Captain Jean-Luc Picard, who finds a crewman passed out on the floor with a crying baby at her side. He calls for medical assistance, scoops up the baby, and rushes into a turbolift to take it directly to sickbay. With a crash, the lift jolts to a stop. Red alert—the *Enterprise* is under attack. Picard tries to get the lift going again, but the computer doesn't respond. Even though his ship is in danger, he's unable to command his crew, trapped on a turbolift with a &@#&% baby.

On the bridge, Commander William T. Riker tries to

reason with the captain of the attacking vessel, an unknown alien species with a severe case of germophobia. The alien shakes a bag of etched marble sensor readings at him—she knows the crew's infected, she's seen this virus before: it's unstoppable. The alien captain won't allow the *Enterprise* to enter their space without a fight. Suppressing a cough, Riker explains that they're not sick; it's probably just allergies—didn't they get the notification of the high pollen alert today for this sector? Suspicious, but also sensitive to pollen, the alien captain lifts one of her many eyebrows and demands to know if Riker is on any medication for his allergies. Riker claims he is, but that he just stopped taking it, and he promises whatever's going on will be contained to the *Enterprise*. The alien commander doesn't buy it; nobody just stops taking allergy medication. She and her crew can't afford to get sick right before their holiday break. The alien cuts communication and renews her attack.

Meanwhile, in the turbolift, Picard puts the baby on the floor and starts looking for any way out. Nothing. In frustration, he slams his fists into the walls, scaring the baby. He apologizes and cradles it, gently explaining that he hates turbolifts; there's no reason he should be stuck in an elevator on a ship that has to create its own artificial gravity. It's madness. Then he looks on the bright side; this isn't as bad as it could be. Once, he was stuck in a turbolift with Worf, who was all sweaty and grouchy because he had just worked out. At least this is better than that. The baby responds by throwing up on him. Picard tries to keep his cool, but now the kid is just freaking out.

Beverly, in the meantime, discovers she can communicate with the virus using a type of bacterial language. The computer translates the virus's speech for her, so they begin a dialogue. It synthesizes a male human voice with a sensual Spanish accent, apologizing for infecting the *Enterprise* crew, and notes that it finds Beverly very alluring. Perhaps they can continue this conversation over dinner? She is shocked; this virus is totally asking her out. "Huh. Oh, um, sure, what the hell . . ." she mutters. The virus is encouraged: he has read a book on dating and body language and senses she might be into him.

Picard is still trapped, and the baby barf has destroyed his combadge. He's trying to be patient, but the baby won't stop hitting him on the side of the head with a rubber carrot toy. Picard takes the carrot away from it, but it howls a noise that shakes him to his core. He attempts to negotiate with the baby, but it just gets louder and fussier until blood drips out of Picard's ear. He returns the carrot. The kid settles down. Taking the carrot away will not be a mistake he'll make again.

Ten-Forward is mostly empty, except for one table. Beverly, trying to keep a positive attitude about this forced-date, sits across from the virus, which is housed in a Starfleet Medical biohazard container filled with nutrient-rich agar. When it apologizes for being underdressed, she fixes a little bowtie around its container. The speaker attached to the cold, metallic canister offers her a glass of wine. Soon, against all odds, the virus has her laughing and enjoying herself. It recounts adorable stories of resilient creatures it has infected, and expertly lobs some hilarious jokes it learned from some comedians it killed last summer. Beverly can't help herself; this thing has thoroughly charmed her. She agrees to take the container back to her quarters for a drink. The virus is psyched.

Captain Picard rocks back and forth, trying to keep calm. He's covered in thick, translucent infant slime. The baby screams and rasps on the floor of the turbolift. Finally, it falls asleep. Picard sighs and quietly tries to repair his combadge—he drops a wire, which makes the slightest sound as it hits the ground. The baby instantly wakes up and starts screaming louder than ever. Picard starts screaming, too. The combadge starts emitting a shrill error beep. Everyone is screaming.

The icy canister sits at the foot of Beverly's bed, nervously complimenting her décor. Dr. Crusher comes out of the bathroom wearing her regulation Starfleet negligee and cozies up to the virus, admitting that she has a weakness for short replication cycles. She caresses its agar and asks if *it* has any weaknesses. It admits that it's pretty weak against heat, so they'll have to be careful. She immediately slams the medical tumbler's lid shut and taps her combadge—the nurses in the sickbay have been listening in and immediately start synthesizing a heated antiviral for the crew. The virus knows it's been tricked, but it can't be pissed with her. She bested it with her wits, and damn, if that isn't attractive. It tries to seal the deal, but she just isn't interested.

Three hours later, the crew finds Picard and the baby. It's been sleeping for the last hour in his arms, slumber-chewing on Picard's wrist. He silently hands it over to its mother, who says he can babysit for them any time he wants. Everyone around Picard laughs at that, especially Riker. The captain laughs, too, but really he's making a mental note of who's laughing for future punishment.

Memorable Quotes

VIRUS

(flirtatious)

Beverly, your eyes are so green.

CRUSHER

Thank you.

VIRUS

Your lips, they're so pink.

CRUSHER

You're such a charmer.

VIRUS

Your T cells have an abundance of glycoprotein on their surface.

CRUSHER

Swing and a miss.

PICARD

I have spent my entire adult life adhering to the ethical laws and spirit of the United Federation of Planets, but I swear to God if I meet the man who designed turbolifts, I'll plant my foot right up his—

The baby cuts him off with barf-screaming.

Trivia

+ The baby's spit up wasn't actually baby vomit. Elderly man vomit was shipped in from Europe. European barf, especially from the elderly, looks great on camera.

+ The virus's agar was provided by A1 Hollywood Agar, the most popular agar distribution company for film and television. If it's melting under studio lights, then it's not A1 Hollywood Agar, "The Agar of the Stars."

Mistakes and Goofs

+ The sentient virus claims it's into blondes, but Beverly is a redhead. This has been explained in later TNG non-canonical novels: it is referring to her recessive, non-expressed blond DNA. I don't know how people sleep at night without reading the tie-in novels—they fix so many inconsistencies.

+ Worf wasn't supposed to cough in Geordi's face in the opening act; it was a lucky accident that the editors chose to keep it in because Geordi's explosive reaction is such a delight.

The sentient virus's swanky pied-à-terre/highly
secure medical containment container.

"Transporter Madness"

Stardate 48035.3

Commander Worf slowly scans a corridor, irritated because he has a million other things he could be doing, but he's relegated to the unsavory task of tracking down a mysterious noxious odor. Several crew members have lodged complaints about this section of corridor, and Captain Jean-Luc Picard doesn't screw around when something weird is going down on the *Enterprise*—he's learned that every little ignorable weirdness that people report usually ends up being a ship-endangering alien creeper he has to deal with. Better to nip it in the bud before whatever it is takes over half the crew and traps his consciousness in a crystalline pendant, or a wizard's hat, or whatever—he's just riffing, but his intent is clear: make sure there isn't any nonsense going on. Worf begrudgingly checks his scan log: so far, nothing. For a moment, he worries that the smell might be coming from him—after all, he *does* frequent this section of hallway after his work-out sessions . . . activity that can cause him to emit an odor described by some as "disquieting." A quick pit-sniff comes up clear; the smell is not of Klingon origin. But as he's pressing his nose into his underarm, Worf sees something strange: a toe sticking out of the ceiling. A closer inspection reveals that it's wiggling. Worf removes a lighting panel and discovers an ensign whose foot has become literally embedded in the bulkhead above the hallway. He must have been there for a while, because he stinks and keeps whisper-begging Worf for water. Soon, transporter specialist Ridley Roiland helps extract the foot, while explaining that he's seen this type of situation before: it happens when people mess with the transporter and re-phase incorrectly, often merging with other matter in a random part of the ship. He's seen butts get stuck with mattresses, heads combined with hats. Luckily, there haven't been any fatalities, but sickbay is tired of removing people from objects. Worf can't believe anyone could survive being merged with a bulkhead. It used to be a death sentence, but specialist Roiland explains that the transporter safety settings keep the individual cells in a state of flux until they're separated. It's really uncomfortable, and you look like a dork, but you're not going to die.

Soon enough, there's another transporter error—this time a pair of cadets (usually stationed on the *Enterprise*'s lowest deck) are joined at the cellular level with a trash can. As Worf rolls them into sickbay, one of them, Cadet Beckett, admits that their plight is no random accident. They were "buffering." Worf narrows his eyes, shooting *d'k tahgs* at her. Beckett explains that buffering is popular among the lower ranks—it's a recreational transporter program, one that causes a euphoric high by initiating micro-transport hops that force small mistakes in the pattern buffer. These errors get translated into microscopic inconsistencies in brain chemistry, resulting in a high . . . but other times it can go very wrong, re-phasing the user in a shipping container, or halfway through Guinan's hat.

Buffering quickly becomes a dangerous fad aboard the ship—ensigns start phasing in all over the place, freaking out, having bad buffer trips. An entire deck's

worth of young Starfleet crewmen are stuck halfway through bulkheads, doors; one unlucky cadet finds himself staring at the captain, half embedded in the ceiling, one foot in his fish tank.

Worf avoids their flailing as he hunts down the source of the original program—word of his investigation has now spread like wildfire, and people are trying to get in their last buffering hits before he shuts it down. As Worf gets closer to the program's origin point, ensigns start dangerously re-phasing around him. Someone's trying to kill Worf by sending an unwitting ensign to merge with him! Worf runs down the corridors, shoulder-rolling and doing wall jumps to avoid the stoned crewmen appearing in his path. While avoiding cellular combination, he manages to trace the program back to transporter specialist Roiland—the very person who helped him uncover the phenomenon in the first place. Roiland admits that he's been selling the program for months and that there are no Starfleet regulations against his doing so. Worf throws him into the transporter and threatens to buffer *him* permanently unless he deletes the code. He does, and Worf directly beams him into the brig for being such a piece of crap.

While Worf is saving ensigns from their stupid ensign mistakes, Data is worried about the health of his cat, Spot, who hasn't been eating. Wesley proclaims he has just the thing to help: he's been messing around with a strain of DNA for fun that might be of use. It came from a species that loves to eat, so maybe it can improve Spot's appetite. Data doesn't think it's a good idea to inject alien DNA into his pet, but Spot jumps up and eats the sample before Data can protest any further. After an awkward silence, Data and Wes decide they'll just have to see how this one plays out.

Later, Data returns from his duties to find that the door to his quarters is jammed, and he can hear Spot crying inside. He uses his android strength to pry the door open and is presented with a veritable wall of cat fur. The wall falls toward him, numerous cats spilling into the hallway as he tries to wade his way into his room. Data finds that it's filled chest-deep with meowing cats of all sorts of colors and sizes.

Wes arrives to help and admits that the DNA he was messing with was from a tribble. Data finds it hard to process that Wes would experiment with such a hazardous genome. Wes shrugs—once you've spent some time as a being of pure energy, you tend to shoot from the hip with dangerous biology. His powers may have faded away, but he still remembers the rush of turning invisible, the tingle of transferring his electrons across a circuit, the pleasure that comes from being aware of the universe on a higher plane. Data informs Wesley that he must not feel the need to constantly bring up his time as an energy being in all conversations. In some respects, Data himself is an energy being, one that happens to be encased in an

android body . . . and yet he does not make a big deal about it. Wes ignores him: the cats have eaten all the organic matter in his quarters, and now they're moving through the halls looking for more tasty treats. Data and

Wesley need to stop them from multiplying, or the ship is going to be overrun in classic tribble fashion, only this time with claws and cattitude.

The cats have already started moving into their new home and taking over parts of the ship. Engineering is purr central, the brig is wall-to-wall fuzzy tummies, and the walls of Ten-Forward are a mosaic of yowling, clinging felines asserting their territory with puffs of ammonia. The bridge has been hit the worst: there isn't an inch of floor that isn't taken up with toe beans and snoozing kitties. The station chairs are covered with them, and a bunch of chubby ones are sitting on the control panels, batting at the blinking lights. Picard tries to shuffle his way toward his ready room, but the cats all rub against his legs, zapping him with static buildup and knocking him over with their loving enthusiasm. Picard is not amused.

Using various Starfleet-approved cat-capture methods, and being careful to avoid Worf at all costs, Wes and Data manage to herd the cats, now numbering in the thousands, into a docking bay. Wes activates a DNA refraction field, removing the tribble DNA and leaving behind normal cats. They proudly announce to Captain Picard that they've saved the ship, but he reprimands them because he's still covered in cats and what the hell are they going to do with all these damn cats.

A month later, Data and Wesley are able to find a home for the final cat. It's not easy to get people to adopt seven thousand of anything, and even harder to find a home for cats that have tasted running a starship. Now begins the real work: removing cat pee from the carpeted hallways, vacuuming up the mounds of litter and man-sized clumps of hair, and releasing Worf from his allergy chamber hibernation sleep.

Memorable Quotes

WESLEY

Data, I thought you said Commander Riker was in here?

DATA

You are not mistaken, Wesley. When last I left, Commander Riker was sitting right there.

A muffled plea for help comes from under the cats.

DATA

It appears he belongs to the cats now. The adjustment period will be difficult, but one day he will learn to accept his new life.

Worf glares at a bleary-eyed ensign who's combined with the wall in his bathroom.

WORF

Trying to achieve an artificial
high is not befitting of a
Starfleet officer. You have
dishonored your family.

STONED ENSIGN

You got any chips?

WORF

I most certainly do not.

PICARD

*(sitting at his desk
with a cat on his head)*
"Why would I want to run a
beautiful vineyard when I could be
captaining a starship?" I said. And
here I am, covered in a thin layer
of absorbent cat sand.

Trivia

✦ The descendants of the cats in this episode still roam
the Paramount Pictures lot looking for Commander
Riker to this very day. But they won't find him: he's
too fast.

- The scent of cat pee penetrates even the harsh vacuum of space. The urine sun in the Arrar sector can be smelled across the entire Gamma quadrant, and it's only one sun. It only takes one urine sun to ruin a quadrant.

Mistakes and Goofs

- Many of the cats in this episode are obviously children dressed as cats. This is especially evident when one of the cats direct-addresses the camera asking for juice.

Starfleet-Approved Cat Capture Methods

- Gentle phasering.

- Dangle string over Jefferies tube.

- Spin ship so gravity moves them toward a central room.

- Make cooing noises, then shut the door fast.

- Holodogs.

- Get them to run under beds, then one person gets on one side of the bed, and another person gets on the other side of the bed, then you use a tennis racket or one of the longer rifle-style phasers to poke at the cat until it tries to make a run for it, which is when whoever is manning that side of the bed grabs it.

✦ Tiny, cat-sized tractor beams.

✦ Try to throw a shirt over them.

✦ Mouse costume.

The buffering program, available in either mint or lemon flavor.

EPISODE 08·007

"Quantum Dolphins"

Stardate 48115.7

CRASH! The *Enterprise* shudders to a full stop as it strikes something mid-warp. The bridge crew falls to their knees, and everyone in Ten-Forward is soaked in fake alcohol and has to change his or her uniform (which is annoying because laundry day was yesterday). With the starboard nacelle offline, the *Enterprise* is now drifting in space. The repair crew finds something unbelievable in the nacelle's hydrogen intake vent—the body of a glowing dolphin. They rush it to a holding tank set up for just this type of encounter, and marvel that it looks so similar to an earth dolphin. Unlike an earth dolphin, though, this one glows with internal light that looks magical, or like someone built a dolphin with a lightbulb inside, depending on how impressed you are by a glowing dolphin. The crew doesn't have time to enjoy the sight, because the light quickly dims as the mysterious cetacean goes belly up in its tank. Dr. Beverly Crusher was too limited in her knowledge of this species to save its life. Now they must give it a respectful funerary service, where it will be wrapped in newspaper, placed in a pod before the smell kicks in, and then shot into space.

Dr. Crusher shows the captain that her tests on the alien reveal it was no true dolphin, which isn't a surprise, seeing as it was "swimming" in the warp field around the ship (a normal dolphin wouldn't last thirty seconds in the harsh vacuum of space). On the sub-atomic level, it just doesn't adhere to the physical properties of reality; it's a sort of quantum dolphin. Just as Picard is agreeing that this is really weird, both he and the dolphin body disappear from the room in a flash of light. Beverly throws her hands up in annoyance: she's so sick of people disappearing from the ship in a flash of light. It happens with Q, it happens with time travelers, it happens with ghost entities . . . someone needs to figure out how to tweak the damn shields to stop this once and for all.

Swirling in purple fog illuminated by unsettling pink light, Picard finds himself between universes, floating in the coral courtroom of the quantum dolphins; he's on trial for the murder of their friend who was struck by the *Enterprise*. The dolphin prosecutor and judge are both *real* jerks—they make fun of Picard's "wiggly squiggle arms" and his lack of fins. His trial is set for later that day, after the dolphins get some playtime in. This isn't the first, or the second, or even the third time the captain has had to navigate an unsympathetic alien court, which is why he keeps a defense speech pre-written for just such an occasion. He pulls it out, performs a couple of quick edits to fit it to the situation, then makes a mental note to tell Starfleet Academy there should be a class on antagonistic alien courtrooms.

Playtime is over: dolphin court is in session. The prosecutor and judge haven't gotten any nicer; they pretend to be impressed that Picard wants to represent himself, but then one of them slaps his defense speech out of his hands, and the other blows soapy water in his eyes. The captain manages to present an eloquent, convincing argument for his innocence, but the dolphins respond by imitating his voice in an inaccurate/goofy tone. He tries to defend himself again, but the mocking continues. Picard goes silent: he will not stand for this any longer. With the sham trial over, the quantum dolphins admit that they weren't even listening to him, and that he was guilty from the second they saw he wasn't a quantum dolphin. Picard is sentenced to being mushed into chum for the dolphins to feed upon.

As he's about to be dragged away, Picard improvises an amazing eleventh-hour speech, finding a new angle on the evidence that the wounds on the body, along with the damage to the *Enterprise*, completely prove that the dead dolphin was attacking the ship, and technically killed itself while being needlessly aggressive. Picard and his crew not only had nothing to do with it, but they defended their own well-being by not saving the dolphin's life. The quantum dolphins put on a big show of being swayed by this final oration, then laugh at him and jab him with fishbones. They throw him in a pool and force him to perform tricks while their children watch, then dress him in silly clothing and drag him off to a cell to await his chumming while they argue over which quantum wine best pairs with human meat. (It's rosé.)

Picard is given a last meal (a bowl of nothing—the dolphin guard laughs until he cries at this one), then he's led to a chamber that contains the ultimate fate of any criminal in quantum dolphin society: whirling blades that slice you into bite-sized pieces—the Great Chumming Machine. Just before he gets dropped into its yellow, bucket-like maw, Wesley Crusher appears and eliminates Picard's captors. He hopes Picard didn't think he spent his time with the Traveler just goofing around—his powers aren't completely gone just yet. Wesley blasts a wave of energy across the room, scattering the dolphins. Picard is amazed that Wesley always seems to work the Traveler into every conversation. Wesley warns the dolphins not to screw with humans, then teleports back to the *Enterprise* with Picard clinging to his back. The dolphins can dish it out, but they can't take it; they're all grouchy and pissy about Wes ruining their chumming plans. They swear to get their revenge, but they're just yelling at an empty room because their threats can't cross the dimensional barrier. Once they notice this, it gets awkward, and they all agree they should play it off with extra playtime before moving on to other nefarious business.

While Picard is dealing with the scumbag dolphins, Guinan stops cleaning glasses behind the bar in Ten-Forward as she senses something is amiss. She leaves Data in charge (huge mistake) and is drawn to the holodeck, where she comes across a little boy who claims to be lost. Something else is going on here: she senses that, below his childish façade, he harbors great power. She calls out his lies: no child his age could get lost on the *Enterprise*. He admits that he's no ordinary boy—he's a transdimensional trickster named Pho. He's surprised she was able to see through his tricks, especially since she's probably never met an energy being before. Guinan tells him she's met fifteen energy beings. Pho's surprised, but collects himself: he explains that he was sucked into her dimension by a quantum singularity. Guinan thinks it must have happened when they ran over a quantum dolphin, and Pho nods. Yep, that would do it.

Guinan offers to give Pho some hot cocoa while they figure out what to do. The boy's eyes go dark—he already knows what to do. The only way to get back to his dimension is to create another rift in space by destroying the *Enterprise*. Guinan isn't buying it: she can tell this kid is up to no good, and she yells at him to buzz off and not to even think of messing with the ship. He smirks, and says she's right. He doesn't have to destroy anything; he can hop away whenever he wants, but he doesn't want to.

He'll consider leaving in peace . . . if she'll play a game. If he wins, the ship goes boom; if she wins, he'll be on his way. Guinan can't believe she's being dragged into this and reluctantly agrees. She assumes she'll have to play some sort of multi-level chess, or maybe a simulation of an ancient French battle—the usual. Pho hums and concentrates. The corridor disappears, and Guinan finds that they're now in the middle of a darkened hockey stadium, each the captain of his or her own team.

Guinan has never played hockey before, but she's been around the Galaxy a couple times, and it doesn't seem so different from the GiKwari funerary ritual of slap shotting their puck-sized dead into the afterlife, or the goal-tending marriage ceremony of the Hoovo, or how the Boof celebrate the birth of twins by getting into a fight on a frozen lake. Guinan falls back on her experiences, her preternatural balance, and holds her own in the first minutes of the game. Then Pho starts to cheat like crazy: he hovers, makes the puck disappear, and melts the ice under Guinan. Soon she's lost in what hockey fans consider a huge upset (final score 1–0). Pho laughs and boasts that he always wins against foolish mortals—now he's going to destroy the *Enterprise* and there's nothing she can do about it. Guinan rolls her eyes; if the kid had pulled this on Riker, Worf, or even Picard, he might have the advantage. But he played it safe and decided to pick on her, which was a tactical error. He should know when to call it quits and go back to his own dimension. The kid gets huffy—yes, he did trick her, but she still lost. And no mortal just dismisses him. He starts glowing, preparing to destroy the ship. Guinan shrugs—she's not exactly mortal, either. Pho struggles to pull away as she gently takes his hand. He hisses, snaps, and swears at her, revealing his true form (a little lizard dude with bright orange hair). Guinan's hand starts to glow, and the light spreads up to the kid's arm, then to his whole body. He squeaks out "What are you?" just before he scatters into sparkles of light that dissipate into the ether. She coughs and waves his smoky remnants away from her face.

Back in Ten-Forward, Data's glad to see her. He's broken so many bottles, and there's a tiny fire burning in the ice maker. He doesn't know how something that makes cold water could ignite so easily, but Guinan doesn't mind. She easily sets things right, and Data hugs her. He thinks the *Enterprise* is so lucky to have such a great bartender. Guinan smiles and thanks him in her usual *you have no idea what's roiling under the surface of this form, but I really like you, so we're cool* kind of way. Data goes back to his side of the bar while he tells her about how the captain narrowly escaped death at the hands of pan-dimensional quantum dolphins. Guinan pretends that's very exciting.

Memorable Quotes

PICARD

You can't hold all of humanity on trial because we ran over your friend.

DOLPHIN JUDGE

Wade wasn't our friend. He was the worst dolphin of us all.

PICARD

Then why are you holding this sham trial?

DOLPHIN JUDGE

Because we love sham trials almost as much as we love littering.

PICARD'S PUBLIC DEFENDER

I believe it was Butternut, our beloved dophin president, who once said, and I quote, "SQUEEEEEE SQUEEEEE TITTER TITTER CLACK TWEEEEEEEE TWEEEEE CHIRP CHIRP CHIRP TWEEEEEETEEEEEEEEE."

PHO

This ice will spell your doom. In ice.

GUINAN

Can we hurry this up? I need to get back to work.

PHO

No, we can't hurry this up. You're going to be real sorry you treated me like that when—

GUINAN

When you reveal your true power, I got it.

PHO

Stop it!

PICARD

Remember how we found out that warp speed was causing the universe to unravel, or something? That whole thing?

GEORDI

Oh yeah, it damages subspace, right? What ever happened with that?

PICARD

I don't know. We just stopped worrying about it.

GEORDI

Huh. Well, I'm sure it's fine. There's a lot of subspace.

PICARD

It's under regular space, too—it's not like we're ruining regular space.

Trivia

+ The *Enterprise*-D is mostly designed for human-oid use, but it does have two sections designed for aquatic mammals: Cetacean Ops and the Aquatics Bay. Until this episode, the dolphins of the *Enterprise* had never been seen on screen. Few know that both Geordi and Worf were originally supposed to be roommates with main characters that were going to be talking dolphins. The dolphin twins would come in handy on water-covered worlds, and they would rise in the ranks until one was eaten. These stories had to be abandoned when the puppets kept sparking and setting the carpeting on fire. They were cut from the show, and most of their dialogue was rewritten for Troi.

Mistakes and Goofs

+ Riker called the dolphin "a sexy piece of steak." This line should not have been in the show because it's really weird. It slipped into the final cut because the editors had to get to a wedding (out of state) and didn't have time to make sure they'd weeded out all the crazy Riker one-liners that usually end up on the cutting room floor.

The rainbow lines that zoom past the *Enterprise* aren't always stars. Sometimes they're bright planets, horizontal space rainbows, or pods of quantum dolphins.

EPISODE 08·008

"Rikerworld"

Stardate 48118.9

Orbiting a blue star with an unpredictable temporal field, Rastogan-12 is a planet unique for its random fluctuations in space-time and its physical similarity to a doughnut. Due to Rastogan-12's proximity to its sun, the surface of the planet can see time speed ahead thousands of years without any warning, then suddenly slow to a normal crawl. Wesley begs Captain Picard to let him go and perform some experiments on the surface; he's a total fanboy of its unique timeline behaviors. He shows the captain his Rastogan-12 T-shirt and tries to sing him the Rastogan-12 theme song he's been working on. The captain just can't say no to Wes when he makes his big-eyed pleading face, and he allows him to beam a sensor pod down to the barren surface. The pod materializes just as the planet starts to hum, and Wes is excited to see time on Rastogan-12 shoot forward a million years, corroding his sensor pod into a pile of dust. While Wes is irritated that he's lost a perfectly good pod, he's jazzed that he got some cool readings. Amazingly, the surface of Rastogan-12, which was barren five minutes ago, now boasts a lush ecosystem, including humanoids who are genetic variations of Commander William T. Riker.

A world messy with Rikers is something Picard and Riker himself aren't going to ignore. The senior staff beams down to check it out, wearing temporal safety headbands that will transport them back to the ship if a time speed-up is detected. Upon their arrival, the local population goes nuts: it's not every day someone gets to meet their mitochondrial progenitor. Some quick tricorder waving clears up the mystery: one of Riker's skin cells got stuck to the probe when he was up to something in the secluded, somewhat romantically lit cargo bay. In the moments it was on the surface, the cell provided the building blocks for the evolution of all life on the planet. Riker isn't surprised; after all, he's a pretty fertile guy.

Troi and Crusher separate from the group to learn more about life on Rastogan-12: everything, flora and fauna, has evolved from Riker's genes. Dimple-cheeked birds swoop down and cling to muscle trees, blue-eyed rodent creatures swagger and confidently swing their legs over rocks to sit above swaying beardgrass.

Picard and Riker's tour

of the grand Swagger Cathedral is interrupted by beardless Rikers, who throw bags over both their heads and whisk them away to a hidden cavern. The beardless explain there's a fifty-fifty chance of a Riker being born bearded or non-bearded, but the bearded Rikers have been systematically eradicating non-beards in a horrific attempt to cleanse smooth-chinned Rikers from existence.

Having beamed back to the ship, Troi can't concentrate; she has an overwhelming feeling that she's being followed by the spirit of Riker. Beverly thinks it's probably just the William T. pheromones emanating from the planet, or maybe a Scottish ghost. (Dr. Crusher has learned to always investigate the chance that such spirits are involved, just in case.) Their search for a haunted candle or loaf of bread comes up empty and Troi decides to try and sleep it off, but even her dreams are invaded by millions of Rikers. They carry her in a nonstop crowd surf, chanting her name. She mentally spins in a kaleidoscope of muscles and charm.

Picard manages to get representatives of the bearded

and non-bearded Rikers into one room and introduces them to something that neither group had ever encountered before: twentieth-century Earth jazz. At first they ignore the discordant tunes, and it looks like a battle is inevitable, until both groups of Rikers succumb to the silky improvisation and non-traditional beats of the funky-fresh tones. They drop their clubs and axes and immediately start to dance their way toward unification.

In sickbay, Beverly discovers a problem with Troi's hair. Microscopic Rikers are working out on her hair strands, lifting tiny follicle weights and sweating pheromones. Beverly uses medical-strength hair treatment to shampoo the little guys out of Troi's life and down the drain. As she towels off, Troi demands that they make a pact to keep this horrifying turn of events a secret for life. Beverly agrees.

As the *Enterprise* prepares to leave the system, they get a final communication video from the planet. The Riker leaders thank Captain Picard for helping their two groups understand that they should all be one people, united by funk. The leaders expect many years of peace to come from their bass-heavy unification. Right before the end of the message, the image goes crazy as time speeds up. The last ten seconds show the next million years of evolution and history on Rastogan-12. After it's all over, the surface is once again back to being a desolate, lifeless landscape. Wesley and Picard shrug—they know not to get too wound up with time-travel stuff. Captain Picard crosses his legs and orders the helm to set a course: there are reports of a nearby star making a weird noise, and it's not going to investigate itself.

Trivia

+ The Riker Bats that attack the away team in the Manly Mines were bats with fake beards attached. The only way to get a bat to wear a fake beard is to convince female bats that beards are attractive. The TNG crew does whatever it takes to get the job done.

+ Trouble on the set: the Riker cavemen who rode in on Riker Horses had bushy mustaches but no beards. A journalist from *Number One* (the official Commander Riker fan magazine) was covering the shoot, and threw a huge fit that this was non-canonical Riker madness. The crew promptly added some backup beards to the mustachioed Rikers and gave the journalist a latte to calm him down.

✦ The writers originally planned to have this episode take place during medieval times, or during the Wild West era, but then decided just to keep it futuristic. It's really tempting to put episodes in medieval or cowboy times because of all the fun hats wardrobe has in storage. You'd be amazed how much TV is influenced by free hat availability.

✦ Gary Rumbo, one of the head writers on Season 8, had this to say about this episode: "'Rikerworld'—

right. The episode generally works. We enjoyed writing it a lot more than people will enjoy watching it. You know what? That one was for us. We took a gimme on that one. It really wasn't for the viewers." Usually writers get to write one episode a season that tickles them, even if they know everyone else will hate it.

Nothing fluffs up a beard like dealing with a world full of Rikers.

EPISODE 08·009

"The Final Sale Frontier"

Stardate 48121.2

EnyonK, a renowned political strategist from the human settlement on Villia, arrives on the *Enterprise* to work on negotiation tactics with Captain Jean-Luc Picard. He's dragged WhitnE, his beautiful but sullen daughter, along with him, and wow, does she not want to be there. She repeatedly sighs loudly, points out how stupid and boring spaceships are, and bemoans the lack of entertainment. Picard tries to tell her that the *Enterprise* is equipped with holodecks, fitness facilities, scientific wonders: there *has* to be something that catches her interest. She glares at him and says that if it doesn't have shops, then it stinks. Picard sighs: the *Enterprise* doesn't have shops. He asks Wesley to keep WhitnE occupied so he can discuss disarmament treaties with EnyonK without her eye-rolling and complaining.

At first, Wes finds WhitnE annoying. She calls his Mzzk ant farm "lame," and spits gum on the ground while he tries to explain his nanobot-making machine.

She tries to poke its buttons, but he moves her safely away from his lab before she destroys something. He takes her to the holodeck and tries to think about science while she bitterly critiques the view of the Canyons of Trajdor. Just as Wes is about to tell her he has to get back to work, WhitnE suggests they get a better holodeck that can "do music." Now it's time for Wesley to roll *his* eyes: of course the holodeck can "do music." He pulls up a Bach program, but WhitnE shoves Bach off his piano bench and demands *real* music. She has the computer bring up a live show for a Vulcan punk band she likes, Logic Lice. WhitnE is finally impressed—she loves Logic Lice! She and Wes dance to their smash hit song, "The Savage Curtain," and eventually end up making out in the back of the club.

Wes is smitten. Everything he found annoying about WhitnE now seems charming and cool. Donning leather jackets and spiked Vulcan hairdos, they flip through the entire history of Logic Lice, starting with their rocky beginnings all the way to when the band broke up as they ascended into energy beings. Vulcans can choose to dedicate their lives to meditation in an attempt to purge all emotions, a state of mind they call *Kolinahr*, or living with a mind of pure logic. If you're a Vulcan who's really into *Kolinahr*, then you keep meditating even after you've wiped out all emotion, until your body casts off your logic energy and turns to dust. Some argue that this higher level of *Kolinahr* is called "death," but they're just jealous. WhitnE is very impressed that Wes himself spent a summer as a being of pure energy—that is so *Kolinahr* of him. As he walks her back to her quarters he tells her all about how great it felt to be connected to the universe in a way corporeal forms don't allow. She invites him in, claiming that she wants to know more about life as a being of light. Wes doesn't catch her obvious signals for another full hour, when she's forced to tackle him.

The next morning, Wesley goes to his station, light on his feet. Commander Riker knows what that bounce-walk means—he's proud of his young friend. As they head to his lab, Wes tries to describe how great WhitnE is, when an explosion flings them to the ground. Wes runs into his lab and finds his nanobot machine in pieces and WhitnE's leather jacket, now shredded. She must have been poking at buttons on his machine, which always makes stuff blow up. He falls to his knees and starts sobbing, but Riker stops him. He hears something . . . an annoyed sigh? Wes hears it, too. He scans the room and finds a single nanobot that, upon closer inspection, seems bored. Microscopic robots aren't designed for boredom, which means WhitnE wasn't killed—she was transformed into a solitary nanobot. Wes thinks he can bring her back, but he needs some time. Riker offers to make sure the captain and WhitnE's father don't come looking for her; he can stall them. Wes can't believe he would do that, but Riker tips him a wink: he's been in situations like this himself many a time, hoo-boy. Wes doesn't think that can possibly be true, but Riker just winks twice as hard, then runs off.

Riker stops Picard and EnyonK in the hallway outside of Wesley's lab and brags about the captain's amazing fencing skills. Picard is modest, but Riker really lays it on thick. EnyonK is impressed with Picard's ability to see both sides of an argument; he'd love to see Picard behind a saber. Riker ushers them toward the fencing bay— Picard doesn't think they have time for fencing, but Riker claims "no time for fencing" shouldn't be a part of anyone's vocabulary. Picard has to agree, and will allow it.

Meanwhile, Wesley stirs the nanobot into a vat of gray goo while softly singing Logic Lice songs, and soon a human hand emerges. Wes is excited, and he steps back, but the hand grabs his Starfleet-issued nanogoo stir stick and starts to stir itself. Wes tries to grab the stir stick away from it, but the nanobots are too strong.

Soon, Riker pokes his head into the lab and is shocked to find that it's been replaced with a fully operating shopping mall. Stores line the hallway, and a water fountain bubbles beside a vendor hawking fancy hats. Riker finds Wesley hiding behind the haberdasher, frantically scribbling calculations on the ground. Wes explains that the WhitnE nanobot has multiplied, and it has converted the *Enterprise*'s basic materials into its own construct imbued with her sentience: this entire mall is made of WhitnE. Riker begs Wes to think: there has to be a way to take control of this situation before Picard finishes his fencing. Wes is at a loss—WhitnE loves shops, and now she *is* shops. Nothing will turn her back into a human.

Riker has an idea: What if they *out-shop her . . . ?*

After a moment of silence, both Wes and Riker shriek in delight at this amazing plan.

In a flurry of conspicuous consumption, the two go on a wild spending montage. They try on a bunch of outfits, mixing and matching flamboyant shirts, pants, shoes, and jackets. They pig out at the food court, get their ears pierced at a store called "Brittney's," then cover themselves in gaudy bling. Soon, laden with bags, they blow credits at the candy store when they hear the mall moan. "It's working! We can do this!"

They amp it up and shop even harder, buying sporting goods, pets, padds, and porcelain figurines of children fishing. Clutching a newly purchased crystal goose, Wes notices that the walls are starting to melt. "We're almost there!" Riker is worried—there's nothing else to buy. Wes theorizes that if there's anything malls hate, it's when people keep their receipts. He holds up a giant pile of them, and the two start returning stuff. The mall starts to crumble, and soon morphs back into the form of a single person. Wes and Riker toss her into a hastily constructed re-humanizing machine and flip the switch . . . just as Picard and EnyonK walk into the lab. Picard is in the process of apologizing to the ambassador, who is now sporting an eye patch. EnyonK demands to know where his daughter is, because he wants to leave this instant. WhitnE pops out of the re-humanizing machine, smiling and cheerful, and definitely no longer comprised of nanobots. She hugs her dad, and kisses him on the cheek and thanks him for bringing her on such a fun trip. EnyonK softens and tells Picard he will be using all of the political strategies they discussed . . . and forgives the captain for stabbing him in the eye. It was a fair duel, after all.

Riker and Wes chuckle as EnyonK and WhitnE beam back to their ship, and admit, "That was a close one." Picard asks them what they mean, and they turn, surprised, because they didn't know he was there. Riker tries to fabricate some nonsense about how he and Wes are intellectually invested in disarmament treaties, but Picard waves them away like stinky air: honestly, he doesn't want to hear it, as he really doesn't care.

While Wesley is navigating the labyrinth of space love, fan-favorite Miles O'Brien is back for a visit. He's been enjoying a happier, more involved life on Deep Space 9, where he actually gets to go on adventures and be a functioning part of the decision-making. Sure, he ends up getting captured, shot, tortured, and wrongly imprisoned more than ever before, but at least he isn't treated like a part of the background. Now he's here to deliver a case of yamok sauce to Guinan and spend the night before returning to his own show. Geordi and Data, well versed in his harsh tone and quick temper, are amazed to find that (against previous experience) O'Brien is now genial and friendly. Gone are the days where he would sneer at Data and pretend that Geordi didn't exist. Now he's all smiles, wants to hang out with them, and even offers to host a poker game. Apparently, being stationed by a wormhole has warmed the icy heart of the *Enterprise*'s surliest crewman.

Exhausted from their long evening of gambling and raunchy storytelling with O'Brien, Geordi heads off to bed, but Data refuses to leave; he wants to chill with O'Brien for the rest of the night. Hours later, O'Brien finally loses it: no more knock-knock jokes, no more games of "what animal am I thinking of?" He is *done* with the android. He kicks over his couch while Data cowers against a wall. O'Brien's been trying to get rid of him all night, but Data just can't take a hint. O'Brien climbs up on the couch and unscrews a ceiling panel. Back in the day, he hid a bunch of Picard's expensive stuff here, which he'd stolen while the captain was stuck on a turbolift. There's a couple of statues, a rare bottle of wine, a ball of Spock's hair—all sorts of goodies. The whole night was a sham: O'Brien was just being nice so they wouldn't be suspicious, but obviously he underestimated how numb Geordi and Data are to social cues. He slides a couple of boxes full of ancient alien artifacts out of the ceiling, then he stalks out of the room. Data begs him to stop—they

can still be friends, right? Data assures him he can keep this a secret, but O'Brien doesn't care. He hates the *Enterprise*, he hates the stupid control panel in the transporter bay that he slid up and down day in and day out. They never appreciated him—he's happier now with a real crew that doesn't get turned into the Borg every other month. He beams out with his stolen goods, laughing so forcefully that little flecks of spittle land on Data's face.

Data vows that he'll prove him wrong, he'll never tell a single soul about O'Brien's thievery. That lasts about thirty minutes—he wakes up Geordi to tell him everything because he's excited to have a secret with his best friend. Then Geordi tells everyone else.

Trivia

+ This isn't the first time an *Enterprise* crewman has accidentally turned his girlfriend into a science experiment. Captain James T. Kirk had a series of girlfriends who ended up getting transformed into gray boxes with colorful crystals sticking out of their lids. It was a simpler time.

Mistakes and Goofs

+ O'Brien yells "Don't point that thing at me!" and throws a haphazard punch at the camera operator in the scene where he falls through Geordi's Popsicle stick art. Geordi is a brilliant engineer and would never construct such shoddy work.

While Wes only has his memories of WhitnE, Riker got to keep this shuttlecraft she sold him with only .5 percent APR for twelve months.

EPISODE 08·010

"Deadly Cadence"

Stardate 48125.6

Worf is miffed: he planned to spend his day off learning new tumble-fighting moves and sharpening his *bat'leths*. Instead, he has to give a tour of the *Enterprise* to Gla'ar, a visiting Klingon who's famous for his antagonistic poetry. He's also renowned for developing his signature screaming meter (high-pitched, low-pitched, low-pitched, high-pitched) and considered a living treasure in galactic reading circles. Gla'ar is one tough Klingon, and he thinks Worf is an idiot and a traitor for serving on a Federation starship. He has his assistant spit in Worf's face. Worf balls his fists but calms down when he catches Picard's *a Starfleet officer wouldn't punch a guest* look. Worf contains his rage, adjusts his outfit, and mutters to himself. Gla'ar is a fundamentalist Klingon—he follows the ancient ways that most Klingons have forgone for modern life. Gla'ar doesn't wash his hands after going to the bathroom, he lets paper cuts become dangerously infected, and he knocks other people's items off of their shelves for no reason.

(He literally wanders through other people's quarters and throws their personal belongings onto the floor, claiming it's a "super-ancient" Klingon tradition, which Worf suspects he's making up; he's never heard of this particular tradition, but he doesn't want to chance being wrong about it.) All of Gla'ar's beliefs center around the ancient Klingon desire to constantly prove to yourself and to the gods that you're the toughest *Suvwl'* on the block, even if that means pissing everyone else off. Worf spends his entire shift following Gla'ar around, patiently keeping his mouth shut as the creep disrupts random crewmen with his screaming and bullying.

The second day of Worf's chaperoning duties proves to be unnecessary when he finds Gla'ar dead in his guest quarters, half his body lying through a shattered glass coffee table.

After calling for medical assistance, Worf rubs his temples: this isn't going to be an easy case. The list of suspects is pretty much anyone Gla'ar has ever met. With all the bureaucratic red tape and the honor battles this will instigate, it could take months to sort out.

Captain Picard hates when their missions of exploration are interrupted by Klingon drama, but he's ordered by higher-ups at Starfleet Command to keep the Empire happy by allowing a Klingon investigative team to board the *Enterprise*. Each missing an eye, and all distinctly grouchy looking, the investigators immediately get to work. As they move Gla'ar's body, they find something hidden underneath: a poem he's hastily scrawled on the carpet in his own blood, just before death, that clearly accuses someone:

Worf IS MY DESTROYER
Let us know, my Worf, that you are the softest
  Klingon of all time
Softer than A JUVENILE TARG
Worf's hands are pillows, his cranial ridge jiggles

HE set me on fire and threw me through HIS
coffee table.
The SOFT ONE finally shows some spine.

The Klingon investigators seal off the crime scene, claiming they must ensure Federation allies of the accused don't have a chance to tamper with the evidence. Picard thinks that's ridiculous, but the Klingons scoff at his naïveté: it's what the Federation would do if the situation were reversed.

With insulting poetic evidence pointing against Worf, the Klingon investigators sentence him to execution. Their judgment is bound by Klingon law, which allows for the ritualized killing of anyone who murders a poet, artist, or any Klingon whose profession is of a non-deadly nature. None of the investigators had read Gla'ar's poems, but they're not ones to pass up an excuse for a death ritual. Picard is all for diplomacy, but he'll be damned if he's going to let a bunch of smarmy Klingon blowhards rush through an investigation just to bully their way into killing one of his senior officers. He pores over Gla'ar's oeuvre, looking for any clue to prove Worf's innocence before the executors arrive on the *Enterprise*. Gla'ar spent so much time writing insulting poetry that there might just be some indication of who had motive to kill him. Unfortunately, Gla'ar is no G'Trok; most of his poems are lazy and meandering and lean heavily on how much he liked blood. A sampling:

Yum blood
Most delicious blood
The only thing better than blood is MORE blood

and

Let us drink Cortack Blood, my g'r, and let it be
*   spilled*
For we have but two lives to consume blood, this
*   one and the next*
I wish I had a better kut'luch
I WOULD USE IT TO MURDER KAR'MAR
KAR'MAR is ugly and his wife has weak hands
And then we could spend the evenings drinking his
*   blood*

Soon enough, a robed Klingon blade squad arrives and prepares its ceremonial stabbing tools. By this point, Picard has read tons of poems about kill-parties and blood showers, but nothing that proves Worf's innocence. Counselor Troi has to hold Commander Riker back as the hooded Klingons take Worf away. Geordi begs the captain to do something, but Picard is tied by his obligations to Starfleet regulation. One executioner comments on how ironic it is that Worf is just like the main character in Gla'ar's play. Picard is shocked: Gla'ar wrote a play? He digs it up and discovers that it's a pedestrian and over-explainy work, and the plot revolves around a Klingon poet who constantly lies about liking blood, and who frames a Starfleet officer to bolster his reputation and poetry sales. Worf is taken aback: Who doesn't like blood?

Picard orders a search of the ship, and soon Commander Riker finds Gla'ar alive and hiding in the cargo bay, eating cake. The executioners are shocked to see that it's *not* blood cake. This is a huge no-no. The blade squad escorts Gla'ar to their ship. He's going back to Qo'noS to answer for his cakey crimes. Picard wants to know if they're going to punish him for trying to frame Worf, too, but they ignore him.

While Worf deals with his libelous laureate, Data and Geordi have the time of their lives on a two-man away mission to the lush planet Luvu. They're excited that they don't have any higher-ranking commanders with them—this time *they're* in charge! They get their work done quickly so they can have a little fun exploring the planet before they have to report back to the ship. Data finds something crazy: a Tangorian wasp hive. Geordi yells, "No way!" and they hide behind some bushes and bug out their eyes as they stare at the wasps; they're totally freaking out over how cool and scary they are. Tangorian wasps are pretty much like Earth wasps, but they have an extra stinger that makes getting stung hurt twice as much. This is according to Geordi, who said he heard it from a guy at engineering camp. Data is very impressed. They carefully back away from the wasps, respecting their double stingers.

Later, Data and Geordi are back on the ship, and they head to engineering, where Data makes a horrifying discovery: there's a Tangorian wasp on Geordi's back. Data immediately evacuates the room and seals the doors. Geordi trembles and holds as motionless as possible, begging Data to get it before he gets double stung. Data attempts to use his android speed and anti-sting skin to pluck the wasp from his friend, but can't because it's vanished. Data and Geordi crouch on the ground and look around; it could be anywhere. Carefully, they search the room, each holding a plastic cup to catch it if it buzzes up. Geordi spots the wasp cleaning its creepy antennae on the master systems display and acts fast: he roars, closes his eyes, and dives at the tiny monster with his cup held high. He opens one eye and smiles: victory—he's trapped it! His celebrations dim as he realizes that he miscalculated his dive attack. He's accidentally got his cup and the wasp planted firmly on Data's chest. The wasp attacks the inside of the cup as Geordi and Data cry in despair.

An hour later, things haven't gotten better. Geordi and Data try not to panic, but it's getting harder as the bug gets angrier. They've managed to slide the cup off of Data and onto the ground, but the wasp is *pissed*. They extend the warp containment field around the cup, raise the neutrino emissions to placate the wasp (it's not working), and consider going back in time to stop themselves from messing with the hive in the first place.

Sure, Data's time machine is extremely dangerous, untested, and was purchased from a sketchy vendor on Risa who approached them on the beach with a cooler full of time machines, but on the other hand: this thing has *two stingers*. While the guys are planning to endanger the time-space continuum, Dr. Beverly Crusher comes in with a sheet of paper, slides it under the cup, and takes the wasp to the transporter room to beam it back down to Luvu. After all this panic, it's obvious that Geordi and Data won't be going on missions without a commanding officer anytime soon, but they're actually fine with that because the last couple hours have been way too scary.

Memorable Quotes

GLA'AR

I love blood! I love drinking it,
bathing in it, writing with it,
sprinkling it on things just for
fun.

WORF

I also love blood.

GLA'AR

Not as much as me.

WORF

I do! I love, uh, drinking blood.
Yum!

(drinks a little blood, gags)

Yum.

DATA

Geordi, I am experiencing a general
sense of disquiet. I am concerned
that this is a situation from which
I will never escape.

GEORDI

Don't freak out on me, Data.

DATA

Geordi—if I die, please delete the file in my logs labeled "Notes 2."

GEORDI

I really don't want to be hearing this.

DATA

Geordi, do not look in the file. It does not . . . actually contain *notes*.

GEORDI

Oh, man. I don't want to know. Please don't tell me.

Trivia

+ Some of the Tangorian wasps used in this episode were actually licorice gummy bears, which are almost as disgusting as real wasps.

+ The long string of expletives Data yells when he stubs his knee were dubbed in post to a string of *Star Trek*–style technobabble that almost, but doesn't quite, make sense in the scene.

+ The producers wanted Mark Twain to show up in this one, but they couldn't figure out how to logically make it happen. Nothing says *Star Trek* like Mark Twain. Nothing.

+ All blood consumed by Klingons in any *Star Trek* episode is never real blood, and if it were, they would never admit it.

Mistakes and Goofs

+ When Gla'ar describes his use of "allusionary" imagery, what he meant to say was "illusionary" imagery. I mean, come on, Gla'ar, have some grammar honor.

+ When Worf and Gla'ar visit Chaucer on the holodeck, Chaucer is very inaccurate. Chaucer didn't wear Rollerblades, never said "Yo yo yo, dudes," and most certainly could not flip a BMW over a river, as he does multiple times in his scene. This entire sequence could have been cut for time, but that was an expensive BMW and a hard shot to get. If you spend three weeks and a BMW on a scene, you better believe it's going to stay in the episode.

Can you find the wasp lurking in engineering?

EPISODE 08·011

"Fertile Ground"

Stardate 48126.9

There's a laundry list of important work for the crew of the starship *Enterprise* to attend to. Captain Jean-Luc Picard has a schedule that runs the gamut from taking readings of a mysterious "on-again/off-again" star to checking in on a science station where he's pretty sure the staff have turned into statues, monsters, "or some such nonsense." All that goes out the window, though, because, before they can jump to warp, a blue-and-purple free-floating crystal that looks like someone clipped off a piece of the Crystalline Entity and repurposed it for this episode comes drifting into their sensor range. Unlike the Crystalline Entity, this crystal doesn't have an agenda, but it does have a humanoid trapped inside. Picard loves unexplained crystals. He can't resist examining it, even though history has shown that there has never been a positive result for Starfleet ships that do so. But look how blue, purple, and mysterious it is: it's too tempting. He abandons his busy schedule and orders Data to go ahead and investigate the sucker.

They pull the mysterious object into the shuttlebay, where it immediately melts into a pile of crystalline goo, leaving behind a humanoid woman named Antoinette, a horticulturalist who got herself trapped inside the thing when she investigated it years ago. Picard is psyched: he knew investigating a crystal was going to eventually pay off. Everyone is so caught up with the new guest that nobody notices that something else is forming in the now-forgotten goo. (If you hate suspense and want to know what it is, just skip the next paragraph.)

Antoinette is amazed at her new surroundings and allows the captain to escort her to sickbay. A beautiful woman of science who also shares an interest in mysterious crystals? Picard's curiosity has been aroused. He escapes the pressures of commanding the *Enterprise* by spending time with Antoinette in the hydroponics bay, where she likes to hang out under the grow lights, drink water, and cool her feet in a tray of delicious soil. Beverly pretends to organize her neurocortical monitors while she jealously watches them strike up a whirlwind romance. She can't help but get pissed at Picard for falling for another alien woman, even though it's pretty obvious there's going to be a shocking reveal later in the episode that Antoinette's an alien plant. Picard ignores how Antoinette keeps commenting on how her roots feel, her constant praise of all the hard work that bees do, and how she occasionally coughs up pinecones.

With plans to take her dancing at the Moulin Rouge and horseback riding on a holodeck deserted island, Picard encounters a giant, translucent caterpillar-esque creature still covered in the crystal goo. He tries to fight it off, but the thing is just too gooey; every punch is softened, every phaser blast is scattered by the crystalline structure. Antoinette finds them in the throes of battle and saves Picard from its prismatic mandibles by metamorphosing into her full plant-like form. She sprays the alien caterpillar with anti-pillar chemicals. It bursts into flames, turns into a column of ash, then explodes. Satisfied and spent, she collapses in Picard's arms. Riker meanwhile can't get over how awesome that caterpillar death was. Turned into ash AND exploded? That was very impressive.

Embarrassed that he was avoiding the crew for so long, and more than a little ashamed of his plant-love, Picard makes sure Antoinette is rehabilitated by the hydroponics technicians and has her transplanted to a nearby M-class planet with lots of indirect sunlight and water. She apologizes for keeping her plant-nature secret, but she admits that she wasn't trying very hard to keep it under wraps. Picard shrugs: if he questioned every mysterious woman in his life, he'd never get out of his ready room. Beverly smirks as Antoinette beams away. New love interests may come and go, but Dr. Crusher is always a couple of decks away. She pops her blue medical jacket's collar and struts back to sickbay.

Unaware of Picard's blossoming romance, Geordi is miffed because he can't get any work done—not with this pesky mouse that keeps pulling wires and plasma modules out of his workstation. He's had enough; he's a graduate of Starfleet Academy, the chief engineer of the Federation's flagship, and he will *not* allow himself to be bested by a critter that solves most of its problems through gnawing. He and Data set a series of increasingly elaborate traps to try and catch it.

The first is a simple snare, set up in the hallway outside engineering, baited with a zesty apple pie. The mouse rides the snare, using it to attack passing crewmen as it eats the pie bite by bite.

The second trap is more elaborate: Geordi designs a pressure plate that activates if a mouse-weight sits on it. He scatters them throughout a couple decks that have been seeing increased rodent activity. When activated, the plates create a localized attenuated linear graviton beam that immobilizes the rodent, and then a targeted micro-transport beam phases the mouse away from the plate and into a bucket Data has filled with wood chips and stuff to chew on. The mouse gathers all the bait from the pressure plate traps, altering its weight by carrying a ball of Worf's shedding on its back. (Worf blows his coat on a bimonthly basis, which is why his hair always looks so shiny.) The traps get more elaborate, incorporating the best tech the ship has to offer, and some that hasn't even been tested yet, but the little thing keeps outsmarting them. Data thinks it's time to ignore the mouse and focus on their usual duties, but Geordi is in it to win it.

Geordi starts to go a little crazy from lack of sleep and hallucinates that the rest of the crew are giant mice who are laughing and holding their bellies. In his vision, he's trapped in a mirrored labyrinth being chased by a mustachioed mouse that mocks him for being a human loser. The dream renews Geordi's focus, and he starts to get frighteningly obsessed with capturing the mouse.

Data is worried about his friend who no longer sleeps, and whom he has caught hitting a block of cheese with a hammer.

Geordi snaps, and he sets up his most dangerous trap yet. He kicks everyone off deck twenty-five and slowly decompresses each room, driving the mouse into a torpedo launching bay. Things go south when Geordi and the mouse both get stuck in the slowly decompressing hyperbaric chamber; he and the rodent are going to asphyxiate together. Trapped in close proximity, Geordi discovers that it's really a mouse-like alien with hyper intelligence, six legs, three extra eyes, and the ability to turn invisible. These abilities explain why it hasn't been tricked by any of his traps, but it doesn't make him like it. Geordi and the mouse of unknown origin are going to live a while longer: the creature burrows into the door mechanism and strips the wires so Geordi can reroute the power. Data wonders if maybe Geordi has learned a valuable lesson from his rodent friend about working together, not judging a book by its cover, and maybe even finding big friends in small packages. Geordi rolls his eyes: he hasn't learned any lesson at all. He heads off to try and capture the damn alien mouse, unaware that it's clinging to the back of his head.

Memorable Quotes

PICARD

If everyone doesn't stop bothering me while I practice my little flute, I'll blow us all into space, and damn the consequences.

PICARD

Antoinette, there's something about you I can't put my finger on . . . you're so full of life; earthy, but complex.

ANTOINETTE

I'm a plant.

PICARD

(laughs)

And what a sense of humor! Kiss me, you rascal.

DATA

Geordi, is it possible that this rodent has a superior intellect?

GEORDI

No way, Data. It's just so small and fast . . . I'll outsmart it, just you watch. Hand me another bowl of those chocolate sprinkles, they help me think.

DATA

I do not understand. To which bowl of chocolate sprinkles do you refer?

(He holds up a small bowl.)
Do you mean this bowl of rodent feces?

GEORDI

Nope, no. No.

DATA

Yes.

Trivia

✦ Instead of using real mice, the production crew saved time by filming a rat from a distance.

* Antoinette's crystal coffin was stolen from a Soviet museum in 1977 and hidden in plain sight on the show.

* If you look closely, in some scenes you can see that Picard's uniform has been drawn on with marker. The crew couldn't find material tight enough for some of the romance scenes.

* For an alien, Antoinette pretty much looked human, except for her green, star-shaped pupils and occasional vines. *Star Trek: The Next Generation* alien effects range from "let's just mess with the pupils" all the way to "let's build an entire bodysuit with makeup and a wig and all sorts of stuff." Messing with pupils and adding some face dots is the cheapest way to make a *Trek* alien, and it takes the least amount of time to get the actors ready for filming. Klingons and Ferengi, on the other end of the spectrum, take forever. The producers knew they didn't have a lot of time to get this episode shot, so Antoinette's original design of "a ten-foot intricately woven bark and flower mosaic" was altered at the last minute to "just do an eye thing."

Mistakes and Goofs

* When Geordi tries to send the mouse back in time, you can distinctly see Riker eating a taco in the

background. This must be a mistake, as it would come with severe diplomatic consequences. Tacos were outlawed by the Federation at the Khitomer Accords. Klingons are offended by any food that provides its own method of containment. The human delegates refused to budge on sandwiches, hot dogs, and ice-cream cones, but conceded on tacos, burritos, and other taco-like meals.

Some of Geordi and Data's Mousetraps

+ An enticing holodeck re-creation of a kitchen full of unsealed boxes and jars, where Geordi and Data hid with katana swords.

+ A tachyon field emitter smeared with honey.

+ Spot the cat.

+ A bowl of grapes balanced with string, so that the mouse would get flipped into a micro black hole hidden underneath.

+ A drawing of an attractive female mouse on the transporter pad, so they could try and beam the little thing off the ship. This failed because the mouse was not a cartoon.

+ A rope trap, devised by the Gorn to capture James Kirk in the Original Series episode "Arena." This didn't work out because a mouse is far smaller than a Kirk.

+ A tube of bamboo filled with diamonds and gunpowder balanced above a door, activated by remote. (Also from "Arena"—Geordi and Data love that episode, and they never pass up a chance to try out the "Arena" tactics.)

+ A box of cookies rigged with a little door that allows one mouse to enter but none to leave. No mice entered, so that didn't work, either.

The phaser's lowest setting is still pretty high to use on a mouse. It's best to hold it as gently as possible, with not more than two fingers.

"White Face Paint and Black Tubing"

Stardate 48128.1

As thanks for repairing their entire political system, the genome artists of Gambier 5 present Captain Jean-Luc Picard with a gift: a perfect clone of Iowa, his favorite childhood horse. To approximate the demeanor of his steed, the Gambierians spent hundreds of hours researching Earth equine breeds, poring over footage of young Picard riding Iowa (which is available to view in Starfleet historical databanks), and accessing interviews with the captain from his Academy days. Picard's at a loss for words: not since a Vulcan ambassador gave him a schooner made of solidified merlot has he been honored with such an erudite and thoughtful gift. Picard hasn't had a lot of stallion-breaking opportunities in recent years—what with all the space exploration—so he's excited to relive a passion from his youth. As he leads the horse toward the holodeck, a slightly less-than-perfect Borg cube appears off the port bow, throwing the *Enterprise* into red alert. Cheap, plastic-looking Borg drones beam onto the bridge and loudly announce, "Uh, so, the Borg are here. Watch out!" Horse training will have to wait. Picard rushes Iowa onto a turbolift, which is a snug fit, just as the ship systems shut down, trapping them inside. Sweating in the

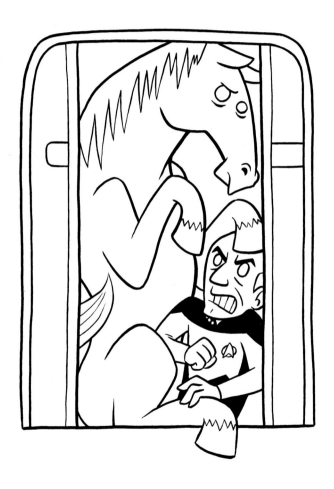

darkened lift, pinned against the wall by a skittish horse, Picard allows himself to wail in despair. How does he always get caught on turbolifts with things? It isn't fair. This never happens to Riker.

There's definitely something fishy going on. Usually, the Borg beam onto the ship and lumber around, bonk into walls, assimilate slower crewmen, and affix black tubing to the walls. These Borg, though, are running at full speed, screaming orders at each other, hissing at the crewmen, and they aren't trying to assimilate anyone, and nobody's trying to attach black tubing to anything. A couple of the drones raid Ten-Forward, drinking straight from bottles as they pack the rest into burlap sacks. Others seem to delight in chasing frightened crewmen away from their posts, just for the hell of it. These aren't subtle personality shifts the crew saw with the splinter Borg cell led by Lore in "Descent." These Borg bicker, cuss, and hit on some of the *Enterprise* personnel. Something is not right.

Before Commander Riker has time to question why the Borg's electronics are taped to their skin, a short Borg "commander" orders him to beam valuables over to their ship. Riker's weirded out; usually the Borg don't care about material possessions, but he's not going to risk the lives of the crew on a hunch. He beams a pile of valuable technological components (and a couple ounces of latinum) over to the Borg cube. As backup Federation ships arrive, the cube hightails it, abandoning the boarding party on the *Enterprise*.

Meanwhile, utterly furious that he's trapped on a turbo-lift again, Picard orders the crew to free him immediately, but they can't hear him over the constant whinnying and grunting of his steed. Picard tries to calm Iowa, gently whispering memories of dressage competitions they used to dominate. Iowa isn't having it: the horse is freaking out, continuously slapping Picard in the face with his mighty tail.

Back on the bridge, a particularly ticked-off Borg pulls off his mask and kicks off his stilts, revealing that he's actually a disguised Ferengi. Sure, there's a treaty with the Ferengi barring this type of acquisition, which is why they dressed up like the Borg. Nothing stands in the way of profit, especially peace agreements. Abandoned by their greedy captain, the boarding team demands that Riker turn over control of the *Enterprise*. Wesley Crusher says he can take them to the battle bridge, which he claims is better than the regular bridge (because *battle* is in the name). He also mentions that it has a special purple laser, which is powered by purple power. The Ferengi think this sounds awesome. Just imagine what they could do with a purple laser! In truth, they don't know what they would do with a purple laser, but it sounds expensive and they want it.

Wes fiddles around with stuff on the battle bridge, stalling for time. He's starting to get nervous that his captors are going to notice that he's been sliding the same system setting up and down for ten minutes—he doesn't

want them getting violent. The Ferengi intruders have no idea what they're doing and are unaware that the battle bridge does not control the ship unless you flip the battle bridge switch, which Wes is making sure not to look at. They tap at non-functional buttons with authority until Captain Picard enters the room on Iowa, tramples a couple of them, and kicks their leader through a wall. He heads to the regular bridge (still on horseback) and commands the crew to track down the fake Borg cube. In awe of Picard's mounted command, the Ferengi return the stolen items. Iowa and Picard eat well that night, and sleep the sleep of victory.

Memorable Quotes

BORG

Put your hands in the air and get on the ground! I'm a Borg and I mean business. I'm talking Borg business, baby!

BORG DRONE

Hey, human. Gimme your pips.

GEORDI

Uh, don't you want to assimilate me?

BORG DRONE

Silence! Move it with the pips.

GEORDI

I'm starting to feel like resistance *isn't* futile.

BORG DRONE

Pfft, whatever that means.

PICARD

(into his communicator)

Number one. I'm trapped on a turbolift with a horse.

RIKER

I can't hear you, sir. Where are you?

PICARD

I have almost become one with the horse.

WES

Shaboomwow, you just got Crushered!

Trivia

✦ Iowa was also slated to appear on *Deep Space Nine* as "Pete the Talking Horse," a regular at Quark's bar. All of his scenes were cut from the final airing of the show because the character's constant one-liners and horse jokes were deemed to be too distracting.

✦ The episode went way over budget because one of the fake Borg drones accidentally fell through a scenic wall. All of the oxygen drained from the ship, and it took an entire day for a specialized team to seal the rip and recompress the set to correct atmospheric levels. This is just one of many hazards presented by filming in space, along with radiation; the high cost of transporting materials, crew, and actor trailers outside of Earth's atmosphere; and the various issues surrounding weightlessness.

✦ This was the cleanest the set ever got. Usually the *Enterprise* had some clutter, but man, they nailed it this day. Just look at those carpets: not a single gum wrapper. Really beautiful work in this episode.

Mistakes and Goofs

✦ The animatronics mechanism controlling Iowa is briefly visible when he's suckling on Picard's scalp.

✦ Riker spit-takes his beer when he sees the Borg cube, even though he had not been drinking anything when it showed up. Tough guys always save a little beer in their cheeks, in case they get surprised by something and need to spit-take in a manly fashion. This is Tough Guy 101, people.

✦ Wesley wasn't supposed to yell "Shaboomwow, you just got Crushered!" in the battle bridge scene, but it was a catchphrase he had been trying to inject into the show since Season 2, and the editors decided this was a bad enough time for it to be featured.

+ We all know that fire can't burn in space, but come on. Like you really want to see phaser battles without fire? You really want to see a Borg cube that doesn't have some satisfying fireballs shooting out the sides? Maybe this isn't the show for you, then.

+ A couple of the background actors are notable because their teeth keep falling out during some of the Borg chase scenes. One of the producers brought in homemade taffy in order to save money on craft services and forced it on the hapless extras, resulting in extraordinary dental bills.

Captain Picard gets a picture with the fake Borg, who are pretending to remember the time he was Locutus.

EPISODE 08·013

"The Lowest Decks"

Dust hangs in the soupy gloom of the uncarpeted corridors of deck forty-three, the *Enterprise*'s least pleasant, lowest area. Dim lights flicker in shadowy sconces, and cobwebbed Jefferies tubes creak and moan. The crew who resides here is the worst of the worst, a collection of ship misfits assigned to the tasks nobody else wants. Duties such as:

- scraping down biomatter junk (sweat, hair, teeth) that gets left behind in the holodeck;

- replacing glass coffee tables when people get thrown through them;

- picking up water cups and candy wrappers from the ready room after meetings;

- and disintegrating hazardous medical waste from the sickbay trash cans.

Creepy, sallow-eyed ensigns Franklin and Lydia are late for their shift again. Both have lazily slept in and groggily pull on uniforms that they haven't bothered cleaning in weeks. Geordi lost at poker last night, so he's been tasked with managing them today. (The senior staff trades off dealing with the lower decks—it's never a fun duty.) He threatens to kick them off the ship if they don't get moving.

The lowest decks might not be pleasant, but the *Enterprise* really is a cush assignment compared to other ships of the line. Franklin and Lydia don't want to lose their positions and end up on some cruddy *Soyuz*-class piece of flying garbage—they get moving and start on their tasks.

Lydia keeps up a constant stream of whining as they go about their duties, while Franklin does the least amount of work possible as he practically sleepwalks through a series of menial repairs. Their conversations revolve around the same three topics: how things would be better if they were in charge, ranking the senior staff by whom they dislike the most, and insulting each other.

About halfway through their usual drudgery, Lydia sprays a month's worth of slime off a holodeck drainage pipe and discovers a Romulan hand imbedded in the muck. Franklin argues that many aliens have hands that look like this one, but Lydia knows that tinge of gray on overly tanned skin when she sees it. She's no dummy: there aren't supposed to be any Romulans on board . . . so

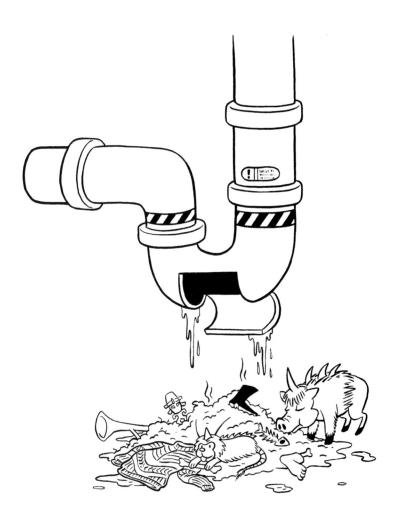

there must be a spy on the ship. He must have gotten his hand lopped off by the organic laser disposal when he was messing around with the holodeck systems; they both laugh while imagining the gruesome scene. Franklin and Lydia agree not to alert Geordi—they're determined to figure out where the spy is on their own so they don't have to admit that they hadn't cleaned out the holo-trap in such a long time.

Franklin tracks the Romulan's DNA using one of his stolen scanners. (Sickbay has so many, so he assumes they won't miss it. This is his general policy on stealing.) They learn that the spy has been attempting to access the ship computer by breaking into icky subsystems that Franklin and Lydia have been neglecting. They find shreds of a shirt tangled in the sewage reclamation pump, a communication ring stuck in the oily wall of a recycling tube, and a shoe lodged in Data's molybedenum-cobalt dump. Lydia's exhausted: they're doing a lot of work to avoid doing work. Franklin says they should look for the spy for ten more minutes, and then they can throw the hand into a turbolift and let someone else deal with it. This conversation ends beneath the transporter room, where they find the spy. He's not a Romulan at all . . . he's a Reman.

[Remans are kind of like less-popular Romulans. They were used by the Romulans as a slave race to dig up dilithium, clean their laundry, be target practice, etc. Remans evolved from ancient Vulcans and look like Vulcans crossed with goblins. (Romulans look like Vulcans crossed with gray couches.) Needless to say, if you're expecting to find a Romulan and instead you get a Reman, you're going to be bummed out.]

Franklin and Lydia walk in on the half-naked, one-handed Reman attempting to break into the transporter lint bin (where all the little bits of crud from the air goes when someone gets beamed in; it's very important to clean this bin BEFORE using the transporter). The two ensigns are so proud of finding the alien spy, and so pre-occupied with arguing about the difference between Romulans and Remans, that they don't notice he's got a phaser in his remaining hand. He disintegrates Franklin, setting off the ship alarms, and takes Lydia hostage.

There's a brief standoff in the docking bay as Worf attempts to negotiate for Lydia's safe release. All seems to be going well until Lydia tries to kill the Reman with

terrible judo. Her lame attempt at throwing him just sends the enemy into a rage. Right before it looks like Lydia faces certain death, Geordi freezes the program. Lydia drops to the floor beside a sheepish Franklin. This was all a holo-test to see if either of them should be promoted one deck up (to forty-two), but Geordi thinks they still have a lot to learn. Franklin rubs his neck, irritated that they fake-killed him again—why do they always fall for these holo-tests? Lydia pitches a quick fit: How are they ever going to know if the ship is actually under attack if every dangerous situation they get into is a holographic sham? Geordi tells them they aren't supposed to be getting in dangerous situations, but they ignore him.

Franklin and Lydia retire to their quarters for the evening, where they talk trash about Geordi and gossip about Riker and Troi.

Memorable Quotes

FRANKLIN

Have you ever emptied the holodeck's biological waste trap after Worf's workout?

LYDIA

Eew, no. What's it like?

FRANKLIN

It's actually kinda nice. Smells
like whisky.

LYDIA

You . . . you haven't tasted it,
though. Right?

FRANKLIN

Oh—oh, no way. Um, that would be
gross.

LYDIA

Good.

FRANKLIN

Yep.

LYDIA

What's that you're drinking right
now?

FRANKLIN

 . . . whisky.

Lydia stares at him as he takes a long sip.

LYDIA

Let's go mess with Picard's fish.

FRANKLIN

No way, that thing is poison. All
those little barbs and stuff?
Poison-tipped.

LYDIA

Don't be a baby. We'll be fine.

FRANKLIN

I've been poisoned before; it's not
fun.

LYDIA

(*mocking impersonation*)
I'm Franklin. I hate being
poisoned.

FRANKLIN

I'm scared of the captain, too. I
mean, the guy has a poisonous fish!
No, thanks.

Trivia

+ A spiritual successor to the Season 7 episode "Lower Decks," "Lowest Decks" highlights some of the only detestable crew members ever seen on a Federation starship who aren't visiting admirals.

+ In all documents, the *Enterprise* is said to have forty-two decks. It's a long-standing Starfleet tradition to omit the lowest deck from crew rosters, design schematics, and official lists—an aesthetic choice to facilitate the ship's seemingly magical ability to deal with trash, sewage, and people who don't fit in.

+ Originally written to be *Star Trek*'s first episode performed live for a studio audience, the format of this one obviously changes back to the normal multi-camera style of filming about a third of the way through. It turned out you need to be able to see the special effects—throwing confetti while spinning in place and yelling "I'm beaming!" just doesn't cut it.

Mistakes and Goofs

+ You can plainly see an uncomfortable boom operator avoiding eye contact with the actors during the creepy sensual trash compactor make-out scene.

+ Franklin misspells Geordi's name in graffiti on the bathroom wall, possibly indicating that he's not such a good reader.

The lower decks crewmen are tasked with cleaning out the hair and bone fragments that this Skull-Faced Monster knocks off of Worf during his Klingon calisthenics program. They repeatedly ask Worf to please take up jogging.

"Terror·forming"

Stardate 48136.3

The *U.S.S. Enterprise* is in orbit above boring old Naldoar Prime. Captain Jean-Luc Picard has been living on the planet for a month, eating its society's unpalatable food and wearing their ill-fitting robes, but it's worth it: he finally negotiates a disarmament treaty between the bickering leaders of the three ruling kingdoms. However, the treaty signing is interrupted when a terrorist from the southernmost nation attacks the Hall of Peace. Picard narrowly makes it back to the *Enterprise* before the warring factions erupt once more: peace has been destroyed, and the planet is doomed. The leaders trigger their super bombs and destroy all life on Naldoar's surface as Picard watches from the captain's chair on the bridge.

Picard hardly has a chance to process what just occurred before a yellow-and-red terraforming ship arrives in the system. It's captained by someone who IDs himself only as Willis, a boisterous, mustachioed terraformer who's inordinately pleased that the world is in need of new plants, water, and chemical elements . . . all products that his company can provide to new settlers. Willis seeds the surface with the building blocks for new vegetation and plops a FOR RENT beacon in orbit.

Suspicious that the guy showed up just before the atomic dust had settled, Picard has the *Enterprise* follow Willis to Hupyria, a planet notable only for its delicious beetles, and has Riker lead an away team to investigate. After a quick bucket of beetles, Riker spies on Willis, who plays the Hupyrian military leaders against each other, and then sells weapons to both sides. Riker tries to calm the leaders down, but they're both fueled by the other's purchase of new ordnance. He tries to explain that they're being manipulated, but they won't listen.

Riker slams the despicable Willis up against the wall of a popular beetle shack and demands to know why he twists peaceful cultures into mutually assured destruction. Willis admits it's all business: he helps vulnerable societies annihilate themselves so he can swoop in and rejuvenate their planets for resale. He pushes himself away from Riker, dusts himself off, then laughs: there's nothing the Federation can do about it; legally he's in the clear. These cultures want to destroy themselves, so he just helps them along. The jerk subsequently packs up his stuff and heads off for the next planet on the brink of war.

The Federation may not be able to stop Willis, but Picard does have Wesley Crusher remotely activate the terraforming equipment in the villain's hold. With his

ship filling with breathable air, potable water, and animals and plants, Willis is forced to beam back down to the Hupyrian surface to avoid being transformed into a shrub or a bird. Although he's temporarily saved himself from being genesised, things aren't much better on the planet: the tensions he's sown have reached a tipping point. The military leaders set off mutually assured destruction. Willis throws both fists above his head and screams into the air as atomic clouds obscure the sky:

"CAAAAAAAAAAAPPPPPPTAAAAAAAAAAAAAAAAA
IIIIIIIINNNNNNNNNNNNNNNNNNN-
JEEEEEEEEEEEEAAAAAAAAAAAAAAAAAANNNNNNN-
NNNNNNN-LUUUUUUUUUUUUUUUUUUU
UUCCCCCCCCCCCCCCCCCCCCCCCCCCC

PIIIIIIIIIIIIIIIIIIIIIIIIIICCCCCCCC
AAAAAAAAAAAAAAAAAAAAAARRRRRRRRRRRRRR
DDDDDDDD!!!!!!"

He doesn't die as fast as he thinks he's going to, and his scream kind of peters out. He glances around, then starts to yell again, "CAPPTAINNNNNNN—" but isn't able to finish the second round of damnation-curse-yelling because an atomic blast turns him into a shadow on the wall of a beetle hut. As the acid rain starts to fall, it's the hardy beetles that are perfectly suited to survive this type of catastrophe. Looks like they just went from being a midnight snack to the top of the food chain.

While Picard and Riker take care of business, Data and Geordi are having their own tough time. They both look terrible—Geordi hasn't slept in days and Data is desperately in need of a recharge cycle. Their wristwatch alarms go off simultaneously; they exchange a frustrated glance, then Data rushes off. He returns a couple minutes later, soaking wet. Worf watches them do this every thirty minutes, for a couple hours, and starts to suspect that they're up to something dishonorable, and probably weird. They're hurrying through duties and turning down birthday party invitations, they show up late and sodden to Wesley's slam poetry recital, and they don't go to Ten-Forward for giant cookie night. Unable to ignore them any longer, Worf snoops and discovers that (of course) they have a quantum dolphin hidden in Geordi's shower. Data has hooked a hose up to the faucet, and they've been spraying the thing down every thirty minutes to keep it alive. The dolphin weakly opens its eyes and thanks them, coughs up some glowing brine, then passes out.

Worf hates aquatic mammals: their constant need to surface for air, their playfulness, their emotional intelligence—he finds it pathetic and weak. A true warrior breathes when he wants, avoids playing, and keeps his emotions locked in a dark little box at the center of his cold heart. The quantum dolphins are even worse—they tried to chum up the captain not too long ago. Worf wants to report the creature to Picard, but Data and Geordi beg him to be cool. They found the poor thing floating in space, run over by a Ferengi pleasure cruiser: they rescued it and named it Zachary. Worf is confident the captain will support their efforts, but Geordi and Data balk: the quantum dolphins don't have a good reputation with Picard. They promise to attend all of Worf's martial arts classes if he keeps quiet. He reluctantly agrees.

Data and Geordi can't handle their duties, Worf's physically taxing classes, and taking care of Zachary, so they start coming up with excuses to get out of their obligation to Worf. As they conspire to hide Zachary in another part of the ship, the dolphin suddenly goes missing. They panic: the rest of the quantum dolphins are going to show up and Picard is *really* going to be ticked off. They decide to run away. Before they can drag their duffel bags to the shuttlebay, Zachary comes splashing into their dimension, fully healed. He thanks them for taking such good care of him, and offers to create anything they want using his powers of matter rearrangement. Geordi and Data know exactly what they want. He smiles and forms two glow-in-the-dark yo-yos for them, then blinks out of reality just before Worf stomps in with Riker, to whom he has one hundred percent squealed. Riker sees no evidence of a hidden quantum dolphin and dresses Worf down in front of Geordi and Data, who wisely avoid snickering. They perform some cool tricks with their new yo-yos, glad that they didn't have to run away . . . yet.

Memorable Quotes

DATA

Come on, Worf. Don't tell the captain.

GEORDI

Worf, please be cool, please? Don't tell. Please?

Worf stares at them for a beat.

WORF

I'm telling.

DATA

Come on!

GEORDI

Don't be like that!

ZACHARY

Be cool, Worf.

WORF

No.

Trivia

+ Zachary's design was provided by Lisa Barney, a popular pencil case and backpack art designer, which explains the rainbow streak running from Zachary's snout to his tail.

+ Young Toby Camworth plays Ensign Roy in this episode. Winner of a bubble gum sweepstakes, Toby got not only a walk-on part, but a picture with the cast and crew, a sack of Riker's hair, and a year's supply of delicious Oh Boy Yummy brand bubble gum.

+ This was the only episode where Worf greeted everyone with a deep, loving kiss on each cheek. Eager to expand the (already popular) Klingon culture, the writers kept adding elements to Worf's behavior that they hoped would round out his backstory. This Klingon practice was abandoned along with the other writer experiments, such as skipping instead of running and the catchphrase rip-off "Well excuuuuuse me!"

Mistakes and Goofs

+ In many scenes, contest winner Toby Camworth can be seen wandering off set, mouthing other actors' lines, and spitting gum on the wall. His performance seems to improve when a series of semi-visible fishing lines appear attached to his clothing, which were used to move him into position. Problems resume when he breaks free of his tethers and runs helter-skelter into other performers. Later, Toby is completely replaced with a life-size cardboard cutout.

Never activate your Genesis Device while driving. Clean out the filter once every three genesises. If you find that your Genesis Device is not terraforming planets, please call the number etched into the chassis.

EPISODE 08·015

"Barclay's Day"

Stardate 48137.1

Lieutenant Reginald Barclay is shocked awake, drenched in a cold sweat. It happened again. The nightmare. Every night, over and over. It always starts the same—things are going fine, and then he steams himself to death in a shoddily constructed sauna. Every evening, he builds the sauna and, each time, it seals his fate.

Shaking off the memory, Barclay gets up and goes to test out the shoddily constructed sauna he's secretly built in his quarters. He daydreams of inviting the captain in for a steam, buddying up, talking shop, and sweating out their stress in a couple high-thread-count Andorian towels. Excited to form that friendship, Barclay takes the sauna for a test spin. He quickly traps himself inside. As he bangs on the door, yelling for help, Q and his cohort, California Steve (another entity from the Continuum), appear in a flash of light, just out of Barclay's view, and shake their heads in disbelief. They can't believe it's happening again: Barclay's going to expire in his sauna for what's likely the hundredth time.

Although all of the Q are called Q, some of them like to choose nicknames for themselves. California Steve is that kind of entity. He picked that name out all by himself, and he's really proud of it. One time, California Steve turned an entire planet into felt because its global emperor made fun of his name. He's the first to admit that he overreacted, and he really should have just forced their ruling class to fight each other to the death in a booby-trapped funhouse.

Q and Cali Steve sigh and walk away from the humid mess and down an empty *Enterprise* hallway. They enter Picard's ready room and kick up their feet on his desk while drinking his wine. Q and California Steve have frozen the ship in time to test each *Enterprise* crewman's competence to make sure they're qualified to explore this dangerous region of space. Once a species evolves to a Continuum level, priorities shift, and the temptations and pursuits of corporeal life no longer apply. Beings of this nature usually get their kicks by creating micro-universes, pranking other god-like beings, and testing less-evolved creatures. Q and California Steve are bored with creating micro-universes, so here they are, testing humans once again. The rest of the crew passed its evaluations with ease, but not Barclay. All he has to do is survive a single day without help from other crewmen

and they'll allow the *Enterprise* to continue on its way . . .
but the guy just can't seem to cut it. Until he does, Barclay has to keep living the same day over and over until
he manages to make it through in one piece. They decide
to get moving and start him off on a new day. With a
flash of light, they reset time and watch Barclay once
more. . . .

DAY 103: Barclay locks himself in the sauna again. Q decides to just get rid of it completely: it has to be the sauna's fault; that's the hydro-wrench in the aqua-gears. Once the sauna's gone, Barclay will prove that he's made of sterner stuff. Q is sure of it.

DAY 104: Barclay discovers his sauna is gone. He's worried he won't be able to impress Picard, so he decides to do something else to stand out: clean the windows outside the captain's ready room. Halfway done, he accidentally lets his combadge get sucked off his shirt and into an intake port. Q and California Steve watch as his EVA suit runs out of air. Barclay bangs on the hull, each hit getting softer, until his body drifts silently off into space. Q wonders aloud if Barclay is messing with them.

DAY 109: Barclay presses the wrong set of buttons while trying to create some mood lighting on the bridge. As the saucer section separates from the stardrive portion of the *Enterprise*, he accidentally gets stuck in the dividing hallway and gets split in half by the opposing gravitational forces. On the other hand, he did manage to create a romantic atmosphere.

DAY 212: Barclay tries to learn a magic trick, but gets tangled up in his infinity handkerchief and snaps his neck, which causes him to stumble backward and fall into a maintenance chute, which drops him directly into a bio-matter incinerator.

DAY 344: Barclay stumbles into his replicator, rearranging his skull atoms into a birthday cake.

DAY 1,001: A holodeck arch opens in the middle of Barclay's body, scattering his matter.

DAY 1,430: An endangered space snake injects her eggs into Barclay's chest. The hatchlings eat him from the inside out.

DAY 1,500: Barclay's ear infection spreads to his heart.

DAYS 1,531–1,600: Space snake again.

DAY 1,788: Barclay pulls out a new outfit from a haunted trunk. It unleashes an unspeakable evil that turns his couch into a terrifying creature, which devours him. Q is impressed; he didn't see that one coming. He thought Barclay was going to trap himself in the trunk. This guy is full of surprises.

DAY 5,506: While laughing at how his voice echoes, Barclay falls down a turbolift shaft.

DAY 7,727: Barclay suffers major burns while trying to cook pasta, then locks himself in a trunk.

DAY 8,002: Space snake.

DAY 11,204: Barclay builds his own Geordi VISOR, is blinded by it, and disintegrates his legs while trying to find the light switch.

DAY 20,000: Barclay is back to building the sauna.

Q and Cali Steve are at a loss: they have never seen someone so prone to danger. It's not that Barclay's incompetent; he's actually *amazing* at getting himself killed. California Steve thinks they should trap him in a bottle and take him to show off to the other members of the Continuum, but Q wants to rub it in Picard's face before they do. He pulls the captain out of stasis and brings him up to speed. Picard is not amused that these dangerous and unmerited tests are going on. Q and California Steve tell him to get over it—they'll test whomever they want. Picard knows that fighting their logic will only make things worse, so he leans into their game and asks to spend one minute with Barclay to see if he has any effect on the hapless lieutenant's performance. Q and California Steve scoff, and what follows is a long sequence where Picard patiently waits for them to finish. They make a big show of how they aren't going to stop scoffing, but eventually, they agree to let the captain have a go at it. They drop Picard into Barclay's singular time stream and quietly scoff as they watch.

Picard offers Barclay a friendly word of encouragement and, to Q and California Steve's shock, his day is completely turned around. Barclay's interaction with Picard has washed away any self-doubt; he focuses on his tasks, avoids deadly accidents, and contributes to the ship's successful operation. Picard explains to the higher beings that they've lost sight of what it means to be part of a team. When you can rearrange matter to your whim, you forget that no singular person is on his own in space—it's the crew together that can survive anything, even cooking pasta. Q and California Steve admit that they don't understand humanity's reliance on one another and allow the *Enterprise* to continue on its course. Picard smugly takes a seat at his bridge chair and orders a heading off into the unknown. Within hours, Barclay almost chokes to death on a piece of tape, but nearly a day of intense surgery and some brilliant medical improvisation from Dr. Crusher manage to save his life.

Memorable Quotes

Q

This human loves dying. Being killed is his girlfriend, and he loves her.

CALIFORNIA STEVE

He should marry her. Should we create a humanoid construct out of the concept of death and force him to marry her?

Q

Nah, let's just keep watching.

BARCLAY

I just had the most wonderful dream, where the captain was nice to me, and then I fell into a pit of lava . . . That second part was less wonderful and more burny.

CALIFORNIA STEVE

Wait, how did he even get inside
the shield emitter? That's
impossible.

Q

The guy's an artist. Accidental
death is his canvas.

BARCLAY

My legs! Oh God, my beautiful legs!

BABY SPACE SNAKES

Sssssssss.

BARCLAY

Watch out for the lava, tiny
snakes.

Trivia

✦ The Cowering Strawberry Barclay shape is the only
Star Trek: The Next Generation Children's Chewable
Vitamin® to not include any actual vitamins. It's
pure candy, through and through. The other TNG
vitamins are:

—Banana Facepalm Picard

—Cherry Gowron on a Throne Made of His Enemy's Skulls

—Flavorless White Data

—Grape Darmok, His Omega-3 Held High

—Flavorless White Lore

—Orange Worf Demanding to Return a Broken Sword for a Full Refund Even Though He Doesn't Have a Receipt

Mistakes and Goofs

+ While this episode claims that Barclay's body was torn apart by the magnetic forces of the dividing hallway between the saucer section and the other, goofier-looking part of the ship, in reality his lungs would simply have collapsed while his body froze.

+ Even though the audio cuts out, you can clearly see Barclay mouthing a TV-unsafe expletive while falling into the black hole he created in the docking bay.

+ A space snake would never lay an egg in Barclay— the TNG role-playing game clearly states that space snakes only inject their eggs into giant Gazorpazorpian caterpillars. Duh. You'd think the writers could keep important stuff straight.

Bonus Barclay Deaths from This Episode:

DAY 500: Barclay falls into the warp core while trying to screw the lid on tighter.

DAY 709: Barclay gets his foot stuck in a pumpkin—he's allergic to pumpkin.

DAY 897: Barclay sneezes in the transporter, re-phases without a face.

DAY 1,400: Another transporter error turns Barclay into a mattress. The heat from the transporter sets it/him on fire.

DAY 4,055: Barclay decompresses deck eight while trying to hang a photo of a car and is sucked out of a small hole in the wall through the photo.

DAY 9,920: Barclay dies of thirst, trapped under a barbell in his quarters.

DAY 9,921: Barclay accidentally mails himself to a nearby sun.

DAY 11,203: Barclay tries to "up the range" of his combadge, which explodes on his chest.

DAY 15,500: Barclay has set up his life-size *Enterprise* senior staff mannequin dolls around a meal he's prepared and is serving in the situation room. One of the dolls falls onto a candle, and the resulting inferno destroys the ship. Days later, having managed to survive in an EVA suit, Barclay is pulled into the orbit of a rogue planet. A child on the planet makes a wish upon him as he burns up in the atmosphere.

Day 98: Barclay finds a magic mirror in a forgotten storage bay, showing him the true darkness in his soul. Then he trips and falls on a pair of scissors.

EPISODE 08·016

"Predators"

Stardate 48138.4

The ship is dead silent as everyone performs his or her duties in tense anxiety; they all know that trouble is coming to the *Enterprise*. Troi's mother, Lwaxana, is popping in for a visit. Last time she was on board, Picard had to pretend he owned her to outwit a frisky Ferengi. Her visits are a guaranteed disruption: outfits will be criticized, wall art will be moved around, and someone's going to be the target for her carnal aggression. Deanna scrubs her quarters, hiding any signs of personality her mom might disparage. Picard has set up a secret cubby behind his ready room where he plans to hide until Lwaxana is gone: he crawls in and settles down to catch up on some reading. Data backs himself up; Worf re-oils his already over-oiled swords . . . The stage is set.

Soon enough, Troi's mom swoops onto the ship like a Tavnian buzzard. Within moments, she criticizes her daughter's everything: her lack of a husband, how her uniform fits, the lack of bounciness in her hair curls, and the dullness of her irises. She forces a padd of articles about the dangers of space travel on her daughter, then starts rearranging Deanna's furniture while describing Odo, a security administrator she met on DS9, whom she considers a "fixer-upper." She then demands they all go to bed at 0800 so they can get up early for a workout routine she's devised that includes running naked through dermatologically refreshing cold oat mush. So far, Deanna thinks this has been one of her better visits.

Meanwhile, Wesley Crusher is conducting a series of experiments with ancient DNA. Commander Riker drops in to challenge him to a quick game of tennis. Wes is too busy, but Riker won't take no for an answer. During his flexing, racket spinning, and taunting, one of his sumptuous eyelashes falls into the DNA vat labeled "Velociraptor." Riker really needs to get a handle on his DNA; it gets him into all sorts of plots.

Lwaxana's attendant, Mr. Homn, baby-proofs the bridge under her direction until Troi puts her foot down: her mom needs to cool it and stop assuming that she's having a baby—she's not. Even if she were, the *Enterprise* is a perfectly safe place— BOOM! A sudden explosion rocks the ship. Reports of a monster filter through the crew and alarms start going off. Troi and her mom grab Wesley and crawl into Picard's cubby room with him. He tries to squirm out, but Lwaxana barricades the door; they'll be safe here while security teams patrol for whatever caused the incident. Picard doesn't seem very happy with this plan. Wesley recommends they remain optimistic: if there were a creature on board, he would know about it. He's all about creatures. Lwaxana repeatedly attempts to throw herself into Picard's embrace, but his many hours of holodeck dodge training have finally come in handy, and the captain manages to continuously roll-dodge away from her grasp.

In a darkened corridor, Worf's security team is attacked by a dinosaur/human hybrid that exudes sexuality and fearsome pack-like hunting maneuvers. Wes manages to get a scan of it before it disappears into a Jefferies tube. He realizes with dread that this is all his fault: it's a crea-

ture with the combined DNA of Commander Riker and a velociraptor—a VelociRiker.

The VelociRiker uses its dino-intelligence to systematically destroy the ship's defenses, and it's soon clear that the creature is hunting one person in particular: Deanna Troi. Riker is not going to let this reptilian version of his visage get its claws on his girl, though. He might not be as fast, cunning, or cold-blooded as this thing, but he does have it beat in one category: arm muscles. He lures the beast into Ten-Forward, then challenges it to an arm-wrestling competition. Once it figures out what he wants, the creature agrees. It helps clear a table, and soon man and monster are locked hand in claw in the most noble of competitions. Riker smirks—seriously, there's no way this thing has him beat.

Picard and the Trois barricade the cubby door. After a short time, Riker knocks, in a cheerful mood. He's caught the beast and says it's safe for the humans to come out. They open the door and find that hey, it's not Riker at all—it's the VelociRiker! The hybrid prepares to lunge, but it stops when Lwaxana slaps it. Shocked, the creature backs off. Lwaxana seems to have some sort of power over it. She nags it out of the room, criticizing its scales, then switches tactics and starts professing her love to it. It screeches and backs into a holding cell, where it tries to block the sound of her voice with its claws. The crew finds Riker in Ten-Forward nursing a broken arm. Apparently, he'd underestimated a forearm muscle sixty-five million years in the making.

Captain Picard allows Lwaxana to take the Veloci-Riker back home to Betazed, where she plans to teach it tricks to impress Odo. It manages to scratch a pleading message on the bulkhead, which Picard fails to notice. Lwaxana tugs its leash, excited for the life they're going to build together, and leads it into a shuttle. In the final shot, despair clouds its eyes as the doors shut.

LWAXANA

Sweetheart, don't tell me you still
don't have a man.

TROI

I dated Worf and seriously
considered dating Will's creepy
transporter clone a couple of
times.

LWAXANA

Not good enough. Give me your eggs.
I want to freeze them.

TROI

No. Get off of me.

LWAXANA

Half of those eggs are mine, gimme.

TROI

They are not!

Trivia

✦ The VelociRiker's shriek is a combination of Riker's
voice mixed with a dolphin screech and the word
"yatokach." Later, *Star Trek: Voyager* writers would
reverse the sound to "Chakotay."

- This episode was originally written as a full-length feature script for a *Star Trek: The Next Generation* motion picture. In a rare gaffe, one producer decided that the public wasn't going to be interested in a *Next Generation* movie, or a movie about velociraptors.

Mistakes and Goofs

- The VelociRiker clearly has a piece of toilet paper stuck to its foot while it's reprogramming the holodeck. Awkward.

- Wesley disappears for most of this episode, then shows up near the end with mussed-up hair and lipstick smudges on his uniform.

Worf and Riker hide from Lwaxana on the holodeck.

EPISODE 08-017

"Icy Hot"

Stardate 48139.6

Dressed in puffy Starfleet snowsuits, Commander Riker and an away team have concluded a successful scientific mission on the ice planet Porp. Riker breathes a foggy sigh of relief and kicks his boots up on a chunk of glacier. When ice planets are involved, the odds are pretty high that your away team will get knocked into a crevasse. Not today, though! He's feeling pretty big in his britches—a good commander completes his mission; a *great* one does it without his men falling into a crevasse.

Out of nowhere, a howling blizzard appears and knocks Riker and his away team into a crevasse. The team huddles around their commander; they just have to keep warm until the *Enterprise* can get a lock on their signals, which will be easy as long as unknown life-forms don't attack them. Riker clings to that solace—this is a lifeless planet, so they should remain untouched until help arrives. He may not be a great commander right now, but dammit, he's still a good one.

Without warning, two indigenous ice aliens jump down into the crevasse and drag a crewman out into the blizzard. Dammit. Riker just hates ice planets. He quickly tracks down the aliens and rescues the crewman with some expert *Mok'bara* horizontal flurry kicks. He gets an ice alien in an unbreakable Riker-grip and shakes it for information. Unable to withstand the persuasive shaking, the alien explains that it's a hunter; on this planet, any high temperature is a commodity. It shows him a contraption that sucks the heat right out of Riker's hand. He's in the business of literally hunting down any heat source; he was going to sell the away team's body heat to the highest bidder. Riker narrows his eyes—if they don't get off the planet as soon as possible, they're going to be toast.

Ice toast. As Riker tries to explain what he means, the alien freezes his hand and escapes.

Riker ignores his injury—he can walk it off. What's more important is that the members of the away team need to obscure their body heat and hide from the hunters. Riker and the others cover themselves in glacial dust, which looks like glitter but is actually very serious science dust. They head deeper into the crevasse and are soon chased by a pack of heat hunters. The dust should be working, but the aliens can see Riker, while the rest of the away team is invisible. Riker produces more than double the heat than the other crewmen; there isn't enough glacial dust to cloak his body. Right when he's about to be captured, Riker pulls off his shirt, blinding the aliens with an intense spectrum of chest radiation. They cover their eyes, scream, and fall to the ground—they've evolved to see on the infrared spectrum, but Riker is just too hot. They pass out, overloaded by his awesomeness, and he's able to join his away team just as they're rescued by the *Enterprise*.

While Riker's in trouble, back on the *Enterprise*, Wesley and his crew of lower-ranked engineering buddies flirt with some female ensigns in Ten-Forward over three-dimensional chess. The popular Ensign Vick has agreed to go on a date with Wes, but only if he's completed the Lower Decks Challenge. She explains that it's a series of ship dares that no crewman has ever completed—but if he can do them, she'll give him a chance. Wes is famous for being a genius, a Traveler . . . but can he complete the challenge? Usually, Wes wouldn't get involved with lower-decks hijinks, but it's rare that a girl shows interest in him who isn't an alien or a hologram or something, so he agrees.

Wes loads the list of challenges onto his padd and enlists the help of Geordi and Data to act as coaches. His first challenge is to drink a "Suicide," a beverage made by typing in "everything" on the replicator. Comprised of more than five billion different ingredients from different cultures, time periods, and planets, the Suicide can literally melt the glass it's served in if you don't drink it fast enough. Some have described the flavor as "the physical embodiment of terror" and others call it "too salty." Data takes a step back, announcing that it's overwhelming his sensors. He begs Wes not to drink it, but Ensign Vick is watching, so Wes plugs his nose and downs it. He looks around and smiles—it wasn't so bad. The crowd goes nuts; how did he do it? Wes privately admits to Geordi and Data that he's in over his head—he had a localized transporter stream beam the drink out of his mouth before it got to his stomach. He doesn't want to do any more challenges—that Suicide could have killed him! Geordi and Data shake their heads: it's too late, he can't back out now or everyone will call him a dork. Wes grimly nods: they're right.

Geordi and Data cringe as they watch Wes complete

more dares, each more dangerous than the last, until he reaches the final challenge: streak across the bridge while Captain Picard is on duty. Wes really doesn't want to do that. Really, really, really doesn't want to. Even Ensign Vick is in agreement (she never expected him to go this far), but that just steels his resolve even more. He's lost a lot of his impulsive creativity since his court-martial at Starfleet Academy (all the way back on Stardate 45703.9!). It's time to get some youth back the old-fashioned way: by doing something super stupid.

On the bridge, Picard patiently listens to Fargon, an angry Klingon captain, scream at him over the viewscreen. Fargon's got it in his head that the *Enterprise* was following him and conducting spy operations that go against their treaties. Picard tries to explain that they didn't know they were following him, because Fargon's ship was cloaked, but Fargon isn't buying it. He knows the *Enterprise* crew has never been stymied by cloaking. As much as they complain about other species using the illegal technology, the Federation always has found a quantum beacon or a metaphasic sweep or a tachyon detection grid or a gravitic sensor net or a subspace sensor echo or high concentrations of tetryon particles or distortion waves or an antiproton beam or something to detect a cloaked ship. Fargon is sick of it: they act all high and mighty about refusing to use cloaking tech, but then they also detect cloaked ships without ever using the same tactic twice? That's just showing off. It's infuriating, and this is one Klingon who's not going to take it anymore. Picard gets up out of his chair and delivers a speech so brilliant, ethically nuanced, intellectually persuasive, and emotionally profound that Fargon relents and is about to lower his shields and end his aggression—until a naked, masked man runs onto the bridge, hugs Picard, waggles his butt at the viewscreen, and flees the scene.

Fargon is right back to being furious. Picard sets the ship to yellow alert and orders the naked mystery man to be taken to the brig. With his speech ruined, Picard admits to the Klingon captain that yes, they can detect his ship because the Klingon crew's boastful singing was coming up on their subspace vocalization sensors. They weren't following them and they don't care what he's up to, so Fargon should just calm down. Fargon accepts this explanation and allows the *Enterprise* to leave unharmed while he harshly reprimands his jolly crew. Meanwhile, the streaker is cornered by security, who are ready to phaser/throw a blanket over him. At the last moment, he's joined by a group of naked people all in masks—it's the other ensigns, who are streaking in solidarity. Overwhelmed by the prankish nudity, Worf is unable to apprehend any of them. Wes gets to go on his date, and Geordi and Data get to brag that they're friends with the only guy ever to complete the Lower Decks Challenge.

Other Dares in the Lower Decks Challenge:

* Lick the Warp Core

* Spend One Night on the Haunted Deck 12

* Jefferies Tube Pig Chase

* Spray Paint Your Name on the Main Tractor Beam Emitter

* Leave a Number Two in the Captain's Yacht

* Tip Over a Shuttlecraft

* Do a Kick Flip Over the Upper Phaser Bank

* Spank Worf

Trivia

* Riker's body heat is actually much hotter than this episode indicates—he's so hot they had to tone it back so as not to frighten the audience.

Mistakes and Goofs

* You can clearly see the ice aliens reading magazines, then hiding them when they realize their scene has started.

* The Suicide that Wesley drinks is supposed to have every type of beverage ingredient in it, but you can see that there aren't marshmallows floating on top. Someone obviously overlooked this vital hot cocoa ingredient.

An ice planet crevasse—one of the most popular things to plummet
into on an away mission. Other popular plummet destinations:
bottomless chasm, black hole, gaping maw of a kraken.

EPISODE 08·018

"Hippocratic Style"

Stardate 48139.9

On nights and weekends, Wesley Crusher often roams the Jefferies tubes in search of neat little junctions he can sketch in his diary (everyone needs a hobby). Tonight, he's not alone: Wes stumbles across a stowaway Bolian who, after almost no questioning at all, admits that he's a bounty hunter. His mission: kidnap or kill Dr. Beverly Crusher for Chezzer, a Marmian gangster who runs the Silver Spoon syndicate. Wes is psyched that his mom is famous, but upset that she's marked for death. The Bolian is really, really sorry for hunting his mom: he's pretty bad at bounty hunting, so he probably wouldn't have caught her. In fact, he's poor at hunting in general. The Bolian wishes he hadn't dropped out of law school, but his dad was a bounty hunter, and there was a lot of pressure from the rest of his family to follow in his footsteps, especially around the holidays when they all get together. Wes stuns the guy and drags him out of the tube—he doesn't care about this guy's life decisions; nobody hunts his mom and gets away with it. He immediately turns him in to the captain.

After some gentle interrogation, Captain Picard learns why Beverly has become a target. She saved a Ferengi merchant from drowning a few systems back, unaware that he was being executed for stealing dilithium dust from Chezzer. Assuming that Dr. Crusher is trying to take over his crime empire, Chezzer's put a huge price on her head that's attracting all sorts of unsavory characters.

Case in point: a pair of ships forces the *Enterprise* out of warp and a boarding party beams onto the bridge. It's a group of five scowling mercenaries, working together to capture Beverly and split the bounty.

They are, in order of surliness (surliest to least surly):

✦ **Korpo**—an Aaamazzarite who wields a pair of deadly vibrating nets. Korpo never planned on making a career out of bounty hunting— he just loves the feeling of trapping someone in a net. Not many jobs offer that opportunity other than fishing, which he finds boring. His nets don't need to vibrate per se, it just adds an element of flair that makes him stand out from other net-wielding bounty hunters.

+ **Gorlip**—an Orion with an alien hawk perched on her wrist, which she uses to hunt her prey. Gorlip is always bringing up her hawk, even when nobody wants to talk about it. You're lucky if you get one sentence into a conversation without the damn hawk being mentioned. Even if you're talking about something that has nothing to do with birds, she's really good at steering conversations into hawk areas. She's often seen looking for her hawk, or buying new hawks after she accidentally puts hers through the washing machine.

+ **The Kupow Triplets**—Klingons who all speak at the same time and then awkwardly try to backtrack and let each other have the floor. After seven or eight false starts, they usually just fall into silence. They co-brandish the mega-*bat'leth*, which is just a giant *bat'leth*. Still, a big *bat'leth* is a big *bat'leth*; just because it doesn't have special powers doesn't mean it

isn't a deadly weapon. It takes three Klingons to wield the damn thing, so don't act like you're not impressed.

While the bounty hunters loudly announce their back-

stories and disagree over their plan of attack, Dr. Crusher injects herself with an experimental strength booster: her muscles grow and split her uniform, and her eyes turn jet black. She takes down each villain with medical precision, surgically dismantling their nets, hawk, and giant *bat'leth*, and then beats them in hand-to-hand combat with an array of martial arts moves she dubs "Hippocratic Style." The mercenaries flee, spreading the word that Beverly Crusher isn't an easy target. Captain Picard slaps Beverly on the back: he never knew she had it in her. In response, Beverly picks him up and spins him like a basketball, then throws him across the bridge. The experimental drug has boosted her strength, but it's also heightened her rage.

She tears through the ship, jumps into a shuttlecraft, and takes off in pursuit of the bounty hunters. Riker tries to beam her back aboard, but she evades the ship all the way to Marmi, Chezzer's home planet.

Chezzer, a spindly stick-insect-looking alien, is a hypochondriac crime lord. Everything must be clean and in its place, or he flips out. He's busy having his henchmen wipe down his throne for the fifth time that day when Beverly comes crashing through his wall. Chezzer has no idea what's going on as she picks him up and dunks his head in a toilet. She easily fights off his guards as he shrieks and begs her to dunk him in something more sanitary. To his horror, Picard and Worf beam into his throne room without taking off their shoes. After some pleading, chasing, and cornering, they finally calm Beverly down and manage to pull Chezzer from her clutches. The drug is wearing off, so Beverly is starting to get ahold of herself. She apologizes to Chezzer, who is squirming in a vat of disinfectant. Crying, he tells her that she can have his criminal empire if she'll just leave him alone. She doesn't want to run a mob, but he won't listen. Picard thanks him, and they back out of the room while he scrubs his skin with a metal sponge.

Back on the *Enterprise*, Picard tells Beverly that she has to dismantle the crime syndicate to make up for throwing him around the bridge. She agrees, but she's only going to do it on weekends. Picard is fine with that.

Then they all have tea and play with their new hawk, which Gorlip accidentally left behind.

While Beverly is kicking bounty hunter butt, Geordi and Data are creating their own problems. Their plan of removing the wall between their quarters and bunking their beds in order to get a bigger room isn't working out. Data likes to stay up all night doing complex math problems out loud, while Geordi demands silence at all times because he can literally see the noise. Their bickering gets worse and worse: old arguments resurface and mean-spirited comments start getting tossed around. Data stalks off, wishing that he had never downloaded the program that lets him feel the sting of criticism, and Geordi holds back tears that his so-called best friend could make fun of his inability to get the *Enterprise* up to warp ten without causing a singularity. Later, Data walks in on Geordi doing an impression of him in Ten-Forward and immediately snatches Geordi's VISOR and throws it behind the bar. Pissed, Geordi reattaches his VISOR, then flips open Data's little head flap and dumps a drink into his positronic brain. Data's head sparks and catches fire. He puts it out by jamming his head in a planter and stomps away while Geordi laughs at him. It is *on*.

Both livid and claiming their friendship is over, Data and Geordi start dividing up the ship with a roll of masking tape. Originally, they tried to put down beam emitters, but, really, tape is just perfectly designed to divvy up carpeted hallways. Geordi takes the starboard half while Data takes port. The two have agreed to never cross the line; none of Data's stuff will ever get on Geordi's side and vice versa. It's the end of an era.

About twenty minutes later, both guys are already painfully missing each other. Sick of their moping, and irked that they were too busy squabbling to help capture Beverly when her new powers manifested, Commander Riker pulls the tape up and orders them to figure out a way to work together. Relieved that they can blame Riker for ending their brief feud, Geordi and Data immediately take down their bunk bed and begin building a fort in cargo bay nine. They agree to be best friends forever, but tensions start to rise when they both want the hawk to sit on their respective shoulders.

Memorable Quotes

GEORDI

Maybe you should go and hang out with Barclay in the weirdo club, you weirdo.

DATA

There is no such club as the weirdo club, Geordi. Even a blind man can see that. I say this because I am belittling your affliction.

GEORDI

Low blow, dude.

DATA

Perhaps you should go cry about it to your holodeck girlfriend.

GEORDI
(crying)
Her name is Brooke!

GORLIP

My noble Laaperian hawk will tear your eyes from your skull, human.

                    HAWK
Actually, I won't.

                    GORLIP
We talked about this. . . .

                    HAWK
No, you said we would decide how to
handle this together.

                    GORLIP
We are.

                    HAWK
Really? Then why don't *you* tear her
eyes out?

                    GORLIP
I don't have talons.

                    CRUSHER
Excuse me . . .

                    HAWK
Just a moment, ma'am.

                    GORLIP
You're embarrassing me.

                    HAWK
Good.

                    GORLIP
                (*to Beverly*)
Never get a talking hawk.

Data and Geordi's Secret BFF Journal

A quick scan of Data and Geordi's secret BFF journal provides some telling insights into their relationship:

+ Geordi cleans out Data's lint trap once a week, in private, and never complains.

+ Data knows that Geordi is afraid of tigers, even though Geordi often boasts otherwise.

+ They once threw a jug of milk into a black hole, just to see what would happen, and they are now worried when all the black holes they encounter emanate stinky dairy particles.

+ Both do impersonations of Captain Picard with an Irish accent, which they think is hilarious.

+ Geordi can do a handstand for ten minutes straight with only one break; Data can do it until the end of time.

+ Geordi thinks girls are cool and awesome. Data agrees.

Data activates his irritation subroutines when he finds the less-than-flattering comic book Geordi wrote about him, in which he is portrayed as a big dummy that girls don't like.

EPISODE 08·019

"Tashayarasha Tyar"

Stardate 48140.2

Engrossed with an energy experiment, Wesley Crusher doesn't notice that his framed photo of the captain is dangerously close to falling off a shelf above his workstation. A particularly jaunty song starts up on the galactic radio, causing Wes to jump up and dance around, knocking the picture straight into an active energy beam. The accident causes a feedback loop in his electronics, which quickly spreads out into the *Enterprise*'s main computer systems, frying them at the very moment Picard, Riker, Troi, La Forge, and Dr. Crusher beam back from an away mission. Screaming, they disappear from the transporter pad.

At first, it seems like they'll be lost forever, but Data's hands fly over the transporter controls and he is able to capture their energy signatures in the pattern buffer. Unfortunately, there was only one buffer for five people, and when he energizes them back it combines their DNA into a single entity. Standing on the transporter pad is a man with a combination of all their personalities and physical features: Captain Doctor Lieutenant Commander Picar-iketroi LaCrusher.

The confused being steps off the pad and looks around: he knows this place. He smiles: this is his ship. It doesn't take Data, Wes, and Worf long to decide that they hate Picariketroi. He's a self-obsessed jerk who walks around the *Enterprise* making changes their friends would never allow. He takes down all of Beverly's art and replaces it with his own drawings; he throws out Picard's desk and installs a judo mat. He orders them around in the nastiest, bossiest way. They need to hurry up and devise a way to get their friends separated and back. Picariketroi thinks *they're* all the jerks—he lights a cigar, blows smoke in their faces, and heads to Ten-Forward to relax and hit on "the chicas."

Meanwhile, the *Enterprise* is being monitored from a nearby ship crewed by eight different Tasha Yars (each from a different dimension: see below). Unfortunately, this is quite the unsavory bunch and, boy, do they hate the *Enterprise*. All these Yars are from dimensions where they've been kicked off the *Enterprise* crew, disfigured in

the line of duty, gone rogue, or otherwise been unsuccessful in their Starfleet endeavors. These Tasha Yars have a sinister plan, which begins with their making peaceful contact with the *Enterprise*. At this point, the crew isn't too surprised at seeing a new Tasha Yar show up, even though she died years ago. Sometimes they come across alternate reality Yar daughters who've grown up with the enemy, but most times they run into Yar herself, in alternate timelines (where she wasn't killed on Vagra II). They welcome the Yars with open arms and show them to the suite of rooms usually reserved for visiting Yars. The Yars marvel at Picariketroi, who has Riker's libido, Geordi's love of tinkering, Troi's sweet tooth, Beverly's night vision, and Picard's obsession with privacy. Blind in one eye and with a twinkle in the other, he has Geordi's hair, Beverly's nose, Riker's beard, Picard's torso, and Troi's purple outfit.

Worf and Wesley think that they should trust the newly arrived Tasha Yars, who claim to know how to separate Picariketroi back into the individual entities. Picariketroi is vocal about how *he* thinks the Tasha Yars are full of it, and that their plan is bogus. He can tell the rest of the crew isn't buying it, so he steals a shuttlecraft and tries to flee. He doesn't want to get Tuvixed, no thanks! (Picariketroi is probably referring to Tuvix, a character that appears in the fortieth episode of *Star Trek: Voyager*, which happens on Stardate 49655.2—two years after this episode took place. It is unclear if Picariketroi had some precognition of the event; perhaps he shared a link through the transporter to some non-temporal dimension where people are combined into single entities. It is more likely that the word "tuvix" is also an alien slur, or perhaps being "Tuvixed" is just an unpleasant thing to have happen.)

Wes captures Picariketroi and is about to hand him over to the Yars, until he overhears them planning to kill the being instead of splitting him up into his original components. This is a five-for-one deal to them—they can take out most of the senior crew with a single phaser blast. Data and Wes manage to avoid the Yars and get Picariketroi into the transporter. Re-creating the error that split Riker on Nervala IV (in year 2361, *ST: TNG* Season 6, Episode 24, "Second Chances," on Stardate 46915.2—boo ya), they're able to duplicate Picariketroi, resulting in two identical beings (both curmudgeonly, chain-smoking grumps).

Both Picariketroi LaCrushers think this is awesome and come up with a plan to keep replicating themselves, until Data kicks one of them into the transporter. He runs it in reverse, splitting the duplicate Picariketroi LaCrusher back into his original parts: Picard, Riker, Troi, Crusher, and La Forge. With the room now full of confused Starfleet officers, the Yars pounce. They're evenly matched, and soon the senior staff has wrestled the Yars onto the transporter pad. Picard demands that they end hostilities, but the Yars refuse and renew their attack. One of them accidentally kicks the transporter controller, dematerializing herself and all the other Yars without setting a destination point. Energizing without a target is deadly. Data tries to save them, but, again, he doesn't have time—he can only save one. All the Yars appear on the transporter pad as a single entity: Tashayarasha Tyar: a combination of all eight interdimensional Tasha Yars. Worf sighs and shakes his head: this is going to be a long night. But it's much shorter than Worf thinks, as Tashayarasha and the remaining Picariketroi copy immediately hit it off and start making out. Everyone shudders and looks at the floor; these two are super creepy. Picard gives them a shuttlecraft and tells them to never come back. Picariketroi and Tashayarasha don't care—they think the *Enterprise* crew sucks anyway, and hey, free shuttlecraft.

Memorable Quotes

DATA

Tasha Yar? Again?

TASHA YAR

I'm back, and this time, I'm staying for good!

DATA

Sure you are.

TASHA YAR

What does that mean?

DATA

We just see a lot of Tasha Yars.

TASHA YAR

Do they ever claim that they're staying for good?

DATA

Every single one.

TASHA

Huh. Well, this time *I'm* staying for good!

PICARIKETROI

What are these feelings inside of me? I want a sundae, but I also want to lift weights. I want to crack medical mysteries, but also captain the ship. I feel blind, and I'm mad that Data borrowed my favorite tricorder and never gave it back.

DATA

Ooh! That last part is definitely Geordi.

Trivia

✦ The transporter is designed not to run in reverse because of the potential weaponization of such an ac-

tion. For instance: imagine that you beamed off the ship and then someone reversed your data stream so only half of you reappeared inside-out. That's why there are specific safety guards in place. Data was able to disable the safety function on the reverse switch by shoving his finger under the guard. Please, never do this in real life: safety guards are in place for your protection, and fingers should never be shoved under them.

✦ As stated earlier, this episode is echoed in the beloved "Tuvix" episode of *Star Trek: Voyager*. As viewers are already familiar, the character of Tuvix was a breakaway hit, spawning multiple spinoff series: *Living with Tuvix*, *Tuvix Can't Win*, and *Simply Tuvix*. These were from the same *Star Trek* team who previously brought us the popular characters Picariketroi LaCrusher, Deep Space O'Brien (when Miles had his consciousness combined with the space station's computer), and Cake Troi. With Tuvix, they finally had a hit character that could be spun off for years to come, even though fans universally agree that Deep Space O'Brien was the most nuanced creation and would have made the most interesting lead in a show of his own. Perhaps someday someone will have the courage to show the world what stories can be told when you combine a Cardassian space station with a prickly engineer.

The Eight Tasha Yars

The Tasha Yars in this episode came from eight dimensions, and each has her own distinct personality:

Tasha 1—Grouchy

Tasha 2—Vengeful

Tasha 3—Intense

Tasha 4—Angry

Tasha 5—Irritable

Tasha 6—Hungry

Tasha 7—Testy

Tasha 8—Indignant

Mistakes and Goofs

+ During the big chase sequence down the corridors of the *Enterprise*, the senior staff seems to run through a turn-of-the-century prairie farmhouse. This was a set for *The Bloody Cough*, another (less popular) show shooting on an adjacent stage. Caught up in the moment, the cast actually ran across the Paramount lot, through other stages, out into the street, and down Melrose Avenue. The crew was finally able to stop them at the Santa Monica Pier before they could jump into the ocean. Miles away from the soundstages, and still giddy with a runner's high, the cast and crew abandoned filming for the day and, instead, spent the rest of the night drinking margaritas at Pacos Tacos in Culver City.

Controlling a transporter is sometimes more art than science. If you hear screaming, popping, or crackling, your best bet is to shut it down and blame the other guy.

EPISODE 08·020

"Son of a Mogh"

Stardate 48155.7

Having received dozens of anonymous complaints about behavior and hygiene, Dr. Angelikar Cavallo, a Federation therapist, is tasked with evaluating Lieutenant Commander Worf "son of Mogh" Rozhenko's fitness for duty. Cavallo is a no-nonsense doctor who wears her stuffiness on her sleeve—and that sleeve is drab and practical. She has the power to get Worf kicked off the ship, and even kicked out of Starfleet entirely if she doesn't like what she sees.

The *Enterprise* crew doesn't have time to formally greet Cavallo: during their investigation of an ancient rectangular ship that has drifted into a shipping lane, Wesley Crusher accidentally triggers a dormant program that awakens its computer core. The rectangle ship splits in half, revealing it was actually a massive sarcophagus for a giant alien humanoid. Over a mile long, the creature separates from the ship and drifts toward a nearby Federation colony. Scans reveal that this humanoid is a biomechanical cyborg. If it reaches the colony, it'll consume all organic and inorganic matter in its path to fuel its massive tummy engine.

Dr. Cavallo ignores the giant: it seems like nonsense to her, and (as previously stated) she's NO nonsense. Nothing will distract her from focusing on Worf. Hopefully, she can catch a whiff of the subtle behaviors that are leading to his recent problems with the crew. She heads to Ten-Forward, where, within moments of her arrival, Worf launches into a screaming fit at a waiter who doubts his decorative sash is armor. Worf accidentally stabs the waiter with a broken bottle while gesticulating, then flips his table and storms out. Dr. Cavallo is starting to see the problem.

The titan drifts closer to the colony, lights and mechanical systems booting up along its body. Captain Picard and Data suit up in EVAs and beam themselves directly onto its chest, marveling at their grand view of the nipple-mountains. Defense protocols kick in as they attempt to communicate with it, but menacing cyber crabs, the giant's automated defense units, skitter across its exterior and try to cut open Picard's and Data's EVA suits. Picard kicks them off into space like soccer balls as Data tries to make a digital connection with the big guy. Picard is actually having a good time, even though he's trying to keep a worried look on his face whenever Data turns his way.

Dr. Cavallo interviews various crewmen who have

had issues with Worf. One recounts a transporter error that quickly filled the ship with hundreds of excited dogs. Worf called the dogs "fools" and refused to touch them because they were "disgusting." His suggested solution was to slit their throats, even though the rest of the crew liked them. An ensign explains how Worf has no control over the booming volume of his voice; he once attracted the attention of a hostile species who heard him complaining about the air-conditioning in the exercise rooms. They heard him right through the vacuum of space, his amplitude apparently defeating one of nature's most popular universal laws. Cavallo also interviews some ship teenagers who've had run-ins with the Klingon—Worf hunted them after they dressed as "Worf" for Halloween. He also threatened to rip them into pieces when they found his secret stash of *Pon farr* magazines hidden in a panel above his quarters, and they regularly steal his dirty laundry, which they huff to get high (they call this "Worfing"). Once, Worf bragged for a week about his purchase of a new ceremonial knife, then was never able to fully prove his innocence after a mysterious stabbing.

Meanwhile, as the giant drifts closer to the colony, Captain Picard and Data fight their way to the creature's face and connect to a port on its eye. The creature starts swatting at them with massive fingertips, but they avoid harm by sliding down the eyeball and hiding in its tear ducts.

Back on the *Enterprise*, Dr. Cavallo is not surprised to find that Worf's quarters are a mess. He's ransacked the place, looking for proof that someone's been messing with his stuff. The doctor ignores his fevered searching and asks him why he always orders prune juice and maggots from his replicator when he could be eating something amazing, like period-accurate breakfasts prepared for Napoleon, or a reproduction of Zefram Cochrane's favorite whisky. Worf sneers that Klingons hate creativity and delicious foods, and he shoves day-old fly larvae into his mouth. She wants to know why he has to push the Klingon agenda so hard when he was on Earth for his entire life. Who's he trying to impress? Why does Worf berate his son Alexander for imagined transgressions, even though Worf was absent for most of his life? Alexander was actually raised by a Klingon mother; he's technically more Klingon than Worf.

Now Worf *really* gets upset and yells that he's never wearing Starfleet shoes again and demands that they issue him Klingon boots with the little horns on the ends. He doesn't know what the damn horns are for, but they look cooler than stupid Starfleet shoes. His freak-out reaches a crescendo until he collapses in a heap on his fainting couch. The doctor switches tactics and soon has him relaxing with a couple of blood-wine spritzers. Worf grudgingly admits that he's got problems: he's worried that

honor is subjective, he doesn't love edged weapons, and maggots are gross. He lights a pair of sacred Klingon bone candles and demands that Dr. Cavallo leave him in peace to definitely *not* cry.

Back in space, Picard and Data have managed to climb out of the tear ducts and scurry up into a nostril, which leads straight to the behemoth's biomechanical brain. They kick at its targeting computer until it veers away from the colony and heads toward the only other celestial body—a nearby sun. Picard is bummed that they couldn't deactivate the big guy, but at least he'll finally find peace. The giant starts sizzling as Picard and Data beam to safety.

In Ten-Forward, Dr. Cavallo is preparing to submit her report on Worf to Starfleet when Geordi sits down across from her. In his opinion, there's no such thing as a perfect Starfleet officer; it takes all kinds. Worf doesn't belong to Earth, or Qo'noS. He's got the history of two planets influencing his identity, which can't be easy. The *Enterprise* is on a mission of exploration, and so is Worf. . . . The Klingon's is just harder to see. If you ignore all the yelling, maggot-eating, and sword worship, Worf's a good guy. Cavallo sees the wisdom in Geordi's logic, even as he continues talking and oversells his point. She allows him to ramble as she deletes her negative report.

As Dr. Cavallo is about to leave the *Enterprise*, she gives Worf a final good-bye hug. Worf accidentally stabs her in the arm a little. Embarrassed, he offers to carry her to sickbay, but she sprays on a bandage and tells him not to worry about it. She considers it an honor. He smiles and calls her a fool.

Memorable Quotes

> **DR. CAVALLO**
> What do you see in this inkblot?

> **WORF**
> Regicide.

> **DR. CAVALLO**
> Come on, that wasn't even an inkblot. It was a picture of a dog and a little boy.

> **WORF**
> Damn your trickery.

Trivia

+ Worf doesn't actually eat maggots. He's actually eating caterpillars that have been painted to look like maggots. Which is weird, because they taste worse than maggots.

+ This episode features more stabbings than any other *Star Trek* episode to date, except for the flute stabbing sequence that was deleted from "The Inner Light," which didn't make a lot of sense to begin with.

- The surprising number of tiny background actors in this episode is attributed to Bring Your Child to Work Day. Usually the *Enterprise* isn't crewed by a majority of preteens, but who's going to say no to their kid when they want to be in the show?

- One of the giant's massive eyes was simply a large prop eye the crew found in a Dumpster. What luck! It saved them a ton of time.

Mistakes and Goofs

- The giant cyborg's nipples should have both been hard, or both been soft. Their tendency to get pointy one at a time was weird.

- When Worf tries to stab an imaginary demon with a spoon, you can see that the spoon has a *Made in the U.S.A.* logo. The United States of America doesn't exist in this time period, so it's another job for the Department of Temporal Investigations.

Commander Riker attempts to calm Worf with a hushed lullaby and gentle rocking.

EPISODE 08·021

"Time Fire"

Stardate 48156.3

Captain Jean-Luc Picard kicks his feet up, settles into his favorite chair, and proceeds to spit-take Earl Grey tea all over his pajama pants when Q jumps out of his closet. Dressed in scuba gear and a kimono, he begs for Picard's help, claiming that it's a matter of galactic importance. Picard is immediately suspicious and tries to contact Starfleet Command, but the signal is dead. Q freaks out: of course the signal is dead—everyone is dead! He explains that the Borg are attacking Earth (again), so Picard needs to settle them down the way he does. Picard springs from his chair and agrees to accompany Q, who snaps his fingers and—FLASH!—they're standing on a stone balcony in a desert. Picard is confused: "Where are the Borg . . . ?" Q shushes him. All that Borg stuff was a lie—he actually needs help breaking up with his girlfriend, Cleopatra. Before Picard can process this, the Queen of the Nile herself joins them on the balcony and starts making out with Q, who shoots Picard a "help" look. The captain rolls his eyes and explains to her what a loser Q is and that he wants to dump her. Cleopatra doesn't speak English, but she gets what Picard means from his pantomimes and inflection. Angry and hurt, she calls for her guards, who surround Picard and Q with spears drawn. Q throws an asp at Cleopatra, then—FLASH!—he and the captain are safely back in the future, aboard the *Enterprise*. Q thanks him for handling the situation, kisses him on the lips, runs in a circle, then disappears.

Picard finds Wesley in his quarters and asks him if he could begin work on a weapon that could kill Q. You know . . . just to have, in case. Maybe a katana sword with a quantum edge, or a gun that shoots black holes—Wes should feel free to get creative with it. A glowing rip in space-time appears and almost destroys Wes, who dodges the tear by throwing himself through his experiment-laden table. Agents of the Department of Temporal Investigations come running through the portal in a panic: there's a temporal wildfire spreading across all existence. The DTI has determined that it originated in ancient Egypt and was very likely Picard and Q's fault. The wildfire is going to destroy everything that has ever been and ever will be, and there's nothing they can do to stop it.

The DTI agents climb into clock-shaped escape pods set for a new reality and demand that Picard joins them and that he brings Troi, too, because if they're going to be rebuilding the human race, they want Troi there to help. Picard waves them away and calls for Q to get back here and fix everything. Q reappears, wearing a black graduation cap and robe, and tells Picard to pipe down. But Picard won't have it; it's Q's fault reality is burning. They shouldn't have messed with Cleopatra (Q especially should not have thrown an asp at her). Q claims the only way they can set things straight is by going back and purposefully causing paradoxes. Picard says no way: paradoxes are bad news. Q shakes him. They have to stack paradoxes on paradoxes until they force a crazy paradox-fueled space-time reboot. Q knows it sounds dangerous, but that's because it *is* dangerous. They could be rent apart by a fluctuation in the temporal stream, pieces of their body flung across the central finite curve . . . but it could also be fun. Picard rolls his eyes but agrees to this terrible plan.

FLASH!—Picard and Q are standing in a field at the dawn of man. They shove a couple of cavemen into a tar pit, stamp on some intelligent-looking mammals, then zoom forward in time to hand out shotguns to Neanderthals. They jump forward several hundred thousand years to nineteenth-century France, where they stab Neanderthal Hitler and invent the Internet. They leap forward to the twenty-first century, where Q claims their paradoxes are working—humans never evolved! Picard doesn't share his enthusiasm. They zap a couple of cavemen scientists who are trying to capture them for dissection, then they go forward and blow up robo-Neanderthal JFK's White House.

They leap forward to James T. Cavekirk's eighth birthday and convince him to pursue a career in film criticism instead of Starfleet Academy, then they zip forward a couple decades and give Khan Noonien Cavesingh some extra Genesis Devices.

One final time travel brings them back to their present day, but they've managed to make such a pretzel of space-time that it's unrecognizable. Everyone is a NEWanderthal (an evolved Neanderthal), and while Starfleet still exists, it is now dedicated to setting up coffee shops and tobacco plantations across the Galaxy. Everyone is totally naked, except for wearing heavy, ornate hats that have lots of videos and advertising displayed on multi-angle screens. After hiding their outfits and donning some awkward video hats, Q and Picard sneak around and learn that they're now considered notorious time-villains: a pair of ancient trickster gods who have been messing with Earth since the beginning of recorded history. They fight a one-eyed NEWanderthal Captain William G. Riker, who is in command of the Borg-tech *Enterprise-Z*. (The Borg have allied with the Federation to combat the now universally despised Q and Picard.) Captain Picard and Q blow up the *Enterprise-Z*, then they blow up Earth, and then the sun. Picard is worried that time hasn't fixed itself. They're running out of stuff to blow up when Q decides that *they* need to blow up. Before Picard can disagree, Q grabs a bunch of volatile Eltoniam and—BOOM!

And then

BLOOP.

Time reboots.

Picard looks around. He's in his favorite chair, nestled in his quarters on the regular old *Enterprise*-D with a cup of Earl Grey tea in hand: the same setup from the opening of the episode. He's wearing clothing and doesn't have a horrible video hat. He hides behind his desk and summons Wesley to seriously discuss his ideas for a Q weapon. Wesley thinks the captain is being kinda wonky, but he's not one to turn down fun weapon-design meetings.

Out of the loop on Picard's most excellent adventure, Beverly Crusher and the senior staff are on Bartek-8, a research asteroid, studying exciting cave-escape technology. Starfleet has amazing exploration equipment and techniques, but fifty percent of away-mission injuries are caused by cave-ins, falling rocks, and other subterranean disasters. Hopefully, this new technology will end the current era of cave misfortune.

While testing the equipment, Beverly's assistant is killed in a cave-in and Beverly herself gets trapped under a rock. Beverly rolls her eyes; this isn't the first time something like this has happened to her. She signals for help, but Data and Geordi are trapped in a different cave. Troi and Worf are stuck in yet another cave. Against all odds, Riker *isn't* in a cave. He attempts to rescue Dr. Crusher, but he gets trapped in a cavern, which is really just a wide-mouthed cave.

Beverly activates her highly experimental anti-cave

pants and escapes . . . but is stopped outside by an unexpected figure. It's a future version of herself who has fallen through one of Picard and Q's time rifts. Future Beverly warns her of the folly of her anti-cave pants: they will cause more trouble than they're worth. Away teams *have* to get stuck in caves. Without this final geologic obstacle, Starfleet grows too strong and eventually takes over the universe in a wave of violence. Beverly isn't just changing the fate of humanity—her pants could affect all other sentient races in the Galaxy. (Plus, future Beverly points out that her cave outfit totally looks like "Mom pants"; her usual uniform is way cuter. This may be the future, but "Mom pants" is still a universally reviled style.) That clinches it. Beverly knows she must destroy the pants. She buries them in the one place where they will never be found: in a cave. She rescues the rest of her crewmates with some good old-fashioned rope, then she takes them to Caldos II for some corned beef and cabbage. They manage not to get trapped in any caves, although Data does fall down a well.

Memorable Quotes

BEVERLY

```
It's a time of unimaginable
prosperity. Humanity has solved
all its most self-destructive
```

tendencies. We travel faster than light, instantly translate alien languages, we've conquered the atom—there is no reason we should get trapped in caves and under rocks as often as we do. It's just silly.

As Picard and Q fight their way through a couple of time periods:

PICARD

Time to die!

Q

Looks like it's *death o'clock*!

PICARD

Countdown to destruction!

Q

Uh . . . uh . . . Clock punch!

PICARD

What . . . ?

Q

Yeah, that's a thing. You've never heard of clock punch?

PICARD

That one doesn't count.

Trivia

✦ The *Enterprise*-Z Borg hybrid ship is pretty cool. If you look closely, you can see that it's made of a combination of the *Enterprise*, a Borg cube, and just a tinge of Romulan warbird. Also, there are seven sneakers just painted black, all in a jumble on the back. If you don't lock up your model makers, they'll paint pretty much anything black and throw it onto a Borg cube.

✦ The alternate history Q and Picard create seems pretty intimidating until you get to the TNG era, where everything seems to have evened out to happy times again. It just goes to show you—even if the world were run by half-robot/caveman fascists, things would wind up pretty *Star Trek* in the end anyway. Kinda gives you hope.

Mistakes and Goofs

✦ The sentient cave's sinister laugh was a production choice that the producers regret to this day. There was no reason to personify the cave into a menacing, antagonistic creature. They should have just let it be a cave. Most of the cave's dialogue was left on

the cutting room floor, but the big booming laugh
made it into the final edit.

Dr. Crusher trapped in a cave for a record one hundredth time.

EPISODE 08·022

"Controlled Burn"

Stardate 48158.5

Dr. Beverly Crusher slams her fist on her desk. She and her team have been stymied by a particularly puzzling virus, a heinous biological riddle, for more than a month. Beverly's exasperated: usually it only takes her around forty-six minutes to solve medical problems. Marvista—a planet that is home to the three-eyed Marvistans—is suffering from a worldwide pandemic. Beverly and Wesley Crusher have been working with Marvistan scientists to try to locate a cure, but the world leaders have lost hope. Most of the Marvistan population has visible symptoms (coughing, eyes rolling around, lots of crazy arm wiggling), and this disease is threatening to exterminate their entire species. Few Federation planets are wiped out by viruses—health care just isn't a problem when you can wave electronics over someone's arm to cure terminal illness. Dr. Crusher slams her fist on the desk again: she's determined not to add Marvista to the (very short) failure list.

There's a chance that history could solve this riddle for them. Records indicate that the planet-wide population was almost wiped out more than three thousand years ago, but a small group survived. While flirting with some (sickly) Marvistan archeologists at a dig site, Wesley Crusher unearths an ancient amphora vase covered in medical hieroglyphs that might indicate it contains a vaccine. He rushes it to his mom, who thinks he's saved the planet. Before she can finish her tests on the artifact, a Borg cube arrives in orbit. Beverly slams her fist on her desk for a third time: Again with the Borg? There are so many aliens out there—doesn't anyone else want to assimilate for a while? Wesley doesn't know what to say, and eventually Beverly pulls a small flask out of her inner coat pocket and calms herself down.

Borg drones materialize in town squares all over the planet and start lumbering toward their prey. Unlike on a starship, the Borg have to be patient when they try to assimilate a planet. Sure, they can just carve up the city centers, but it takes a long time to make sure you assimilate all the little nooks and crannies on a continent. If the Marvistans weren't so sick, they would easily outrun the drones, but it's hard to run when you're coughing and dizzy. Beverly and Will defend the hospital in their town, pushing the drones into a river with brooms and garbage can lids. But eventually, they're overwhelmed and have to retreat.

Wes senses foul play, and soon they discover a beacon that's been attracting the Borg, originating from the

planet's capital palace. The Marvistan emperor doesn't care how many times Beverly slams her fist on his desk—he explains that he intentionally signaled the Borg. At least if his people are assimilated into the collective, some part of their DNA will remain in the Galaxy. He wants to preserve the memory of their existence, even if it means losing their free will. Beverly looks around for a desk and, finding none, slams her fist on the floor: How can he be such a pessimist? The emperor doesn't have time to answer as Borg drones bust into his office. Beverly and Wesley need to escape the planet that's now surrounded by brand-new drones with that fresh drone smell. Beverly thinks this sucks and pouts the whole way home, but

Wesley thinks it's kind of cool that the Borg can clean up viruses. He even writes an unpopular journal article titled "Immortality Via Borg." Nobody seems interested in his plan to let sick people get "just a little Borged," so he joins his mother in sulking.

Meanwhile, unaware of Beverly's fist-slamming, Geordi's having a bad day himself due to VISOR problems. At breakfast, his VISOR fell off his face and into his cereal bowl, then it gave him an electric shock when he tried to pluck it out of his milk. Now it's too tight, it smells weird, and the little metal tines keep falling out. After some failed adjustments, he finally takes it to Data, who points out he's been wearing it for the last fifteen years—no wonder it's a piece of junk. Data puts in an order for some newer, cooler VISORs for Geordi to try out.

Soon, the new VISORs arrive and they're actually pretty great. Geordi selects a pair that looks like black 1980s sunglasses, which instantaneously raises his cool factor by more than two hundred percent. Data doesn't want Geordi to feel bad that he's the only guy on the ship who has to wear a VISOR. He has Starfleet ship one out for himself, so now Data can wear it, and now they totally match and look like cool twins! He runs up to Geordi in Ten-Forward and shows off his unneeded VISOR, making a big deal of it. It actually obscures his usually perfect vision, and Data ends up knocking into some tables. People around them snicker, assuming Data is making fun of his buddy. This really heats up Geordi's shorts—he hates that he and Data look like twins now. Data's being a real jerk, as twinning your best friend is not cool. Girls are going to think they're dorks. Besides, Data's the one with glossy skin and fake hair—he already has a thing that sets him apart. Geordi's supposed to be the guy with the cool VISOR—that's the way it's always been! Data doesn't get why Geordi's mad, so he steps up his game. Soon, Data is dressing like Geordi, using his holodeck programs, and ordering his favorite drinks. When Geordi walks in on Data telling one of his classic La Forge family jokes to impress Ensign Vick, he decides enough is enough. Data has to give him his style back, right now. Data balks: maybe he doesn't want to be the pale-gold guy anymore. Geordi shouldn't be such a baby. Guinan gets between them and points out that it's pretty uncool to be jealous. Data admits he downloaded a green-eyed subroutine to see how it felt to covet his neighbors, and that maybe he should dial it back. Geordi apologizes for getting so edgy; he understands that Data's emulation comes from a place of simulated love. Geordi upgrades Data's dancing sub processors, and they wow some deck eight girls with an amazing street-style dance battle. Geordi goes back to wearing his old style of VISOR, and he agrees that Data can wear the cool sunglasses whenever he wants. Worf thinks they should maybe get back to work instead of worrying about what girls think, but, of course, they ignore him.

Memorable Quotes

GEORDI

Ugh! My VISOR fell into the replicator again. And now it's soup. And now I will eat it.

DATA

He is doing it! He is eating his
VISOR!

GEORDI

Ugh! This new VISOR is x-raying
through walls again! I don't
want to see all these ensigns
showering and working out. I can't
concentrate on my work.

RIKER

What a nightmare. Can I try it?

WESLEY

Mom! I think I found a cure to that
disease you've been pounding your
fist about.

DR. CRUSHER

Wes, what did I tell you about
running in the lab?

WES

Yeah, but—

DR. CRUSHER

Go back outside and walk back in
like a professional.

WES

But—

DR. CRUSHER

No buts.

Wes groans, leaves, then walks back in.

WES
(calmly)
I think I found the cur—

DR. CRUSHER
(cutting him off)
Give it to me. Hurry!

Trivia

✦ Yes, those were real Borg in this episode. The crew had to keep the budget tight, and it was easier to use real Borg than build costumes for humans to wear and simulate. A Borg wrangler was on set at all times to ensure both the safety of the crew and to avoid any mistreatment of Borg.

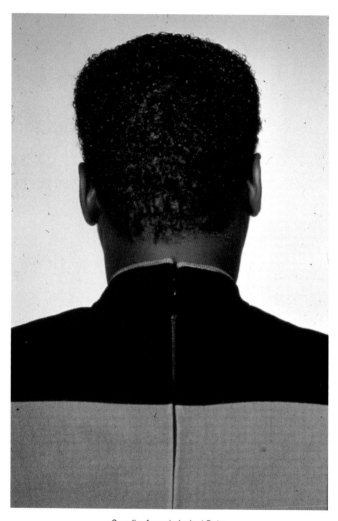

Geordi refuses to look at Data.

EPISODE 08·023

"Pointed Threats"

Stardate 48158.7

In sickbay for a burst blood vessel in his eye, Worf admits he's been screaming at people a little too much lately. Beverly says he's going to have an aneurism if he doesn't calm down, and she just knows he's going to pout for months if that happens. Convinced he needs to relax, Worf packs up his forehead ointment and armor and heads off to the MOFS (Museum of Famous Swords) for some R&R on Zindo, an educational planet in sector 25712. This is a hands-on kind of museum, one that allows visitors to be attacked by someone wielding his favorite swords, knives, or throwing stars. (They sell fun replica swords in the gift shop so one can re-create battles in the privacy of the home.) Within minutes of arriving, Worf already knows the museum is great: he gets to aggressively dodge some weapons he's read about his entire life, he trades honing tips with a couple other visitors, and he geeks out over some fancy scabbards. He would be fully engrossed in the sharpening exhibit were it not for the distraction of Vok

(House of Dink), a young female Klingon who appears to be breaking into the museum's basement archives.

Vok's a reporter—and yes, Klingons have reporters. They try to create the impression that the entire population is made up of warriors, harsh judges, conniving senators, and grouchy generals, but someone has to build the birds-of-prey, mail out the oaths, and keep the lights on. Qo'noS needs its bakers, architects, and livery drivers just like every other planet. So yes, Vok, a Klingon reporter, is investigating claims that Gagliar, an illegal arms merchant from the Siblee sector, is conducting business out of the Museum of Famous Swords. Worf thinks investigative reporting is craven, but he follows her into the archives anyway. They creep around some dusty bins of bow staffs and bolos until they come across a hidden room. Vok's correct—Gagliar and his men are in there, breaking pieces off of Strife, an ancient, particularly powerful sword. Whosoever wields Strife is gifted with strength, agility, and healing powers—the blade literally courses with energy. Gagliar's goons are hitting it with a hammer, scooping up glowing pieces and soldering them onto the blades of cheaper swords. The dimly glowing cheapo weapons are then stacked in wooden crates and covered in packing peanuts. Gagliar is shipping them off-world, pretending that each one is the real Strife so he can sell them at huge mark-ups. Vok is excited: nothing gets Klingon readers riled like ancient swords. Her article about this is going to win her an award. Worf is offended about the disrespect being shown to Strife, and he walks past Vok to brashly confront the perpetrators at the scene of their crime. He and Vok are immediately captured and thrown into a storage closet full of old hilts and cross guards.

Vok and Worf argue, scuffle, then eventually make out. Their passionate thrashing knocks over a pile of daggers, revealing a box of ancient magical swords. (The Demon Blade, The Danger Knife, Garvdo's Revenge, The Singing Sword, and the fan favorite, Old Double Hilt.) Worf and Vok battle their way out of the closet and through a gaggle of villainous henchmen until they reach the leader. Gagliar tries to fight them with the remains of Strife, but he's broken it down into too many pieces—it no longer has the power to defeat their closet-swords. Worf and Vok cut him down, trapping his soul inside the gem in Strife's hilt. (It's super embarrassing to get your soul stuck in a sword.) The power of Gagliar's soul recharges Strife back to its former glory, which pleases Worf as he puts it back in its display case.

Vok invites Worf to join her while she finishes her article by hunting down all the pieces of Strife that had already been sold. They're peppered throughout the Alpha Quadrant and it's going to take some doing to track them all down. When Worf declines, she gifts him a lucky dagger, so he'll remember her every time he stabs someone. Worf awkwardly complains that he already has a lucky dagger, but she just laughs: she thinks Worf's recalcitrant humbuggery is sexy. He calls her "spineless" and runs back to his shuttlecraft while she demands that he call her sometime.

While Worf is avoiding getting his heart cleaved in twain, Wesley is dealing with an entirely different type of heartache. He was totally in love with his alien girlfriend, Brotney, but now he's learned that all his friends were right: she's horrible. Her lengthy, meandering stories about fixing the Bussard ramscoop are excruciating, and she's kind of terrible to his mom. (She calls her "Doctor Dorkus.") Even worse, it doesn't seem like she's going anywhere: she loudly imagines her expensive marriage plans, how she'll paint their future nursery, and what their matching tombstones are going to look like.

Too afraid to break up with her, Wes does some research and learns Brotney's species morphs into a new form when they reach their age of maturity. Instead of dumping her, he's going to wait out the clock until she turns into a tree or something, which is when he assumes their relationship will just kind of fizzle out of its own volition. Data thinks this might be a bad idea and that Wes should just pull the trigger and break up with her now, but there's no changing his mind—this is the perfect plan.

Lo and behold, it seems like Wesley made the right move, because pretty soon Brotney entombs herself in a teal cocoon that's attached to the wall of his quarters.

Wes, Data, and Geordi patiently wait for her to emerge, prepared to either break the news that Wes is breaking up with her, or to fight off whatever monster she's become. Geordi thinks she's going to try to take over the ship; Data's betting she's going to crawl out looking like some sort of crazy snake. Wes doesn't care what she's turned into as long as he can use it as an excuse to free himself from her tender grasp. The cocoon splits down the middle, and she emerges—a much sexier, more adult version of herself. Huh. Geordi, Data, and Wes don't know what to say: they act like complete idiots in her presence, falling over one another to impress her. (Data might not have emotions, but he certainly has mastered the art of "trying too hard." He's been in a holding pattern of sexual awkwardness ever since his Season 1 "fully functional" experience with Tasha Yar; Episode 01-003: "The Naked Now.")

Brotney happily checks out her new form in Wes's mirror—she's pleased with her latest height, hair, and eye color. Wes tries to compliment her, but she cuts him off immediately. Bye, Wesley. Her species evolved to give beta males a chance to pair up with alpha females before they turn into goddesses, but boy did he miss his chance. She hovers off the ground and floats away on a cloud of ethereal light, off to look for a CEO or a professional Parrises squares player to mate with. Wes awkwardly cleans up her cocoon scraps as Data and Geordi tell him not to be too sad: sure she's a goddess who can hover, but she was also a real jerk who they're glad isn't going to be around anymore. They invite him to Ten-Forward to drink apple juice with them and play checkers all night long, just like he used to do when he didn't have a girlfriend. He agrees to go with them, and they have a great time, and nobody goes to their quarters and cries themselves to sleep later. Really.

Memorable Quotes

BROTNEY

Hey, Data—why don't you go download a new face!

WES

(forced laughing)

Oh my gosh, Brotney, that was so funny.

Brotney walks away, heading across the bar to criticize Barclay's outfit.

DATA

I am unable to see the humor in Brotney's malicious insults, Wesley.

WES

She's just joking around, Data.

GEORDI

I think she stinks.

WES

Wasn't your last girlfriend a ghost
that tried to steal your brain?

Data taps his communicator.

DATA

Data to sickbay. Please inform
Dr. Crusher that Geordi just got
burned.

WORF

I haven't had feelings for a woman
like this in years.

VOK

Want to cut ourselves at the same
time with either side of this
warlarK blade, then make out until
we've lost too much blood to stay
conscious?

WORF
(choked up)
You're magnificent.

Famous Swords

Here are just a couple of the famous swords on display at the Museum of Famous Swords:

+ **SnaptroS**—a Klingon *D'k tahg* dagger famous for having been thrown through a rift in space-time to stab its own thrower in the past. T'Kik was a Klingon famous for his knife-throwing skills, but it wasn't until he killed himself on the day he was born that he became a part of Klingon history.

+ **The Pleban**—a Vulcan *lirpa* (a bow staff with a circular knife at one end and a metal ball for bonking your opponent on the other end). A classic "two men enter, one man leaves"–type weapon, most *lirpa*s are used for circle-fighting. The Pleban is famous for being used by various Vulcan warriors in non-circle-constricted battles. Usually, the wielder is quickly taken out with a phaser, leaving behind the signature scorch marks visible on the handle.

+ **Katana**—every ship in Starfleet has a couple of regulation *katana* swords on board. Many space exploration situations call for a ceremonial sword to get the job done; you'd be surprised how often something needs to be sliced in half when you're defending the Prime Directive.

✦ **Mitty**—a *glavin* (Ligonian glove spike) notable for also being handy as a grill tool, because it both spikes meat and protects the hand from open flame. Mitty is famous because it was used to slay Gringar, the Ligonian chancellor who wanted to raise taxes a little too high. Ligonians have a strict set of laws for their rulers, and breaking any one of them means you're going to get a *glavin* right in the face.

Mistakes and Goofs

✦ Brotney appears to be wearing the wrong uniform and rank designation, but this is not a mistake: the costumers decided to have her steal things from other crew members during the episode to accentuate the character's lameness. Her shirt and rank actually belong to Lieutenant Barclay, whom you can see shirtless in the background of some scenes. This also explains why she's got Picard's Dixon Hill hat, a couple of Riker's *horga'hn* statues, and Worf's asthma inhaler.

This Klingon assassin knife was once used to slay three senators in a single day.
It thirsts for blood and requires regular sacrifices to maintain its glossy finish.

EPISODE 08·024

"The Fun *Enterprise*"

Stardate 48159.3

Captain Picard narrows his eyes and slumps in his captaining throne when Worf's cousin Donk uncloaks a stolen ship directly in front of the *Enterprise*. His face fills the viewscreen and he's frantic: he's about to hit ten years old, which is when he has to face the Great Klingon Challenges. The GKC are a coming-of-age ritual that prove young Klinglets are worthy of transitioning to adult Klingon life. Problem is, Donk's been blowing off his challenge classes to hang out with friends. Instead of preparing for the deadly rituals, he's been smoking hand-rolled lizard skin cigarettes behind his battle academy's student graveyard. Now that the challenges are upon him, Donk has no idea what he's doing, and he's afraid he'll be killed without Worf's help. Worf eagerly chastises Donk, whom he's always considered a bit of a dud . . . but the House of Martok family is family; he can't abandon Donk to get destroyed by the challenges. Picard is happy to offer Worf some shore leave to deal with his family affairs, especially since it'll save them all from listening to him snuffle and snort back tears for the next week. Worf thanks the captain, then runs off the bridge and beams over to his cousin's ship.

On Qo'noS, Worf and Donk cobble together matching House of Martok tunics for the challenges. Each youth receives a different set of tasks chosen at random from a giant horrible list that the ruling houses have come up with over the years. The elder Klingons take delight in planning creative horrors for the younger generation—it's half proof of battle acumen, half blatant hazing. Luckily, Donk's list isn't as bad as it could be; Worf thinks he'll be fine.

The next morning, Worf guides Donk through the

drinking, feasting, and *grishnar*-skinning portions of his challenges, and things seem to be going well.

Worf is having fun, Donk is going to survive the challenges, and maybe even be at the top of his class. At dinner, they celebrate with some chalices of *jarzo*, a nasty drink that everyone hates, but it's the traditional Klingon beverage for when things are going your way. Worf's cheerfulness evaporates like water on a hot *targ* when he learns the details of the final test: a human hunt. Worf spit-takes *jarzo* all over the table: he can't hunt a human! He works for humans! He *dates* humans!

Lursa and B'Etor, from the particularly repugnant House of Duras, are running the challenges. (Remember that this episode was shot before the sisters met their end in the feature film *Star Trek Generations*.) They know if Donk fails, he and his family will have to commit shame-suicide. Lursa added the human hunt to the list at the last minute (replacing the classic "cut your own finger off without flinching" test), in hopes that Worf wouldn't have the *toDuj* to help. B'Etor thought it was a good idea and helped out by cackling and steepling her fingers in the background.

Standing on a hover platform overlooking the killing forest, Worf refuses to partake in the hunt. The human Donk has to take down is named Jerry Feldman. He's a friendly Federation civilian who happens to worship Klingons and yearns for a warrior's death. It took a lot of overtime, but Jerry built up enough vacation days to visit the Klingon homeworld to be hunted, and so far he's really been enjoying it. Worf's objections fall on deaf ears and the hunt begins. After beaming down from the platform, Donk quickly trips and tumbles down a ravine, giving Jerry time to get a head start. Feeling the burn of screwing up so early, Donk wrestles his bag of *bat'leth*s out of the gorge, then slips and gets caught in his own nets. Donk begs Worf for help; there has to be some way they can hunt this human without breaking Worf's Starfleet oaths. What if they don't kill the human . . . maybe they can just cut off his legs? Yes, Worf thinks this is an amazing idea. Working together, they quickly corner Jerry, who now thinks this might have been a mistake. It's too late, though: they easily *bat'leth* off his legs, and Donk wins the challenge and preserves his family's lives/honor while becoming an adult Klingon. Worf takes Jerry back to the *Enterprise* to get his legs reattached and to brag about what a great cousin he is. Dr. Crusher is horrified that Worf is proud of cutting off a man's limbs, but she can't stay mad because Worf will be Worf.

While Worf and Donk are thwarting the machinations of the Duras siblings, Geordi and Data won't stop bugging Captain Picard about a pair of items he's been gifted by a visiting chancellor: a particle stick (that can grant wishes by rearranging matter) and a new eighteen-speed bike with a cool red paint job. Riker whistles in admiration: this is a really nice bike. Geordi tries to climb on it, but the captain stands in his way. Picard doesn't want him or Data touching his wishing stick or his new bike. They have a bad reputation when it comes to respecting other people's property—perhaps they remember accidentally shattering his favorite mummy? Geordi argues that the mummy was creeping everyone out anyway, and that they were all having nightmares about it, but Picard doesn't care. They can spend their free time siphoning the warp core, or sprucing up the nacelles: just stay the hell away from his stuff. Geordi and Data wait until he's asleep, then they creep into his quarters and, very quietly, carry his bike into the corridor. The second his door swishes shut, they hop on and co-ride his new bike to a cargo bay where they've built some sweet jumps. It's the perfect fun crime, until, to Data's horror, Geordi accidentally flips the bike and smashes it up pretty badly. Picard's gonna be *pisssseeddd*. Data phasers the remains of the bike, then phasers the phaser to cover his tracks. Geordi groans—he could have fixed it!

Geordi grabs the particle stick and, since neither of them knows exactly what the bike looked like, wishes for it to create their own duplicate *Enterprise*. They can live there and never get yelled at again. Data thinks this is genius. The twin ship materializes in front of the real *Enterprise*, shocking Riker to his feet on the bridge. Why does stuff like this always happen when the captain is reading, napping, or having bathtime? He's never going to give the keys to Riker again if this stuff keeps happening.

The new ship is identical to the *Enterprise*-D, but it has some added flourishes—the nacelles glow a rainbow of colors instead of just blue, there's a T-Rex painted on the hull, and the registry emblazoned on the bow reads "NCC GEORDI AND DATA ROCK 1702-GD." The duplicate ship speeds off, leaving the bridge crew looking to Riker for direction. Commander Riker has a pretty good idea what's happened—this isn't the first time Geordi and Data have tried to run away from the ship when they've been in hot water with their superiors. He sets an intercept course, but he orders the crew to keep it quiet: he doesn't want to wake Picard, or he'll be cranky and they'll all be in trouble. The crew loves Riker, who's both cool and tough: if he wants sneaky, they can give him sneaky. Beverly stands by Picard's quarters, ready to give the alarm if he wakes up. Barclay can hardly contain his excitement: this is awesome.

Geordi and Data are so preoccupied with their fun *Enterprise*—all the arcade machines on the bridge, getting the moves to "YMCA" right (a song that they're repeatedly blaring over the intercom), and keeping the cotton candy machines running—that they don't notice they're heading toward a black hole until it's too late: they get caught in its gravitational influence. Suddenly, having a ship full of plastic balls and free hot dogs doesn't seem so appealing—it's too hard to get the ship under control with all the chaos around them. Geordi tries to get to engineering to super-charge the engines, but they replaced the turbolifts with shark tanks and the Jefferies tubes are clogged with balloons and Silly String. The computer is slow to respond since it's trying to keep all the rides and holographic dancers coordinated: it doesn't have a ton of memory allocated to actually controlling the ship. All is lost, and the fun *Enterprise* starts shuddering and breaking up. Commander Riker manages to beam Geordi and

Data back aboard the less-fun *Enterprise* just as the duplicate ship is violently disintegrated, first turning into a pretty cloud of gray dust, then disappearing into the black hole entirely. Geordi and Data freak out, as the captain's going to be really steamed about the bike. Riker calms them down—he never forgets what a good bike looks like. He uses the wishing stick to re-create it for the captain and even adds a couple improvements of his own (some extra speeds, a bell, and a cool blinking light). They manage to sneak it into the captain's quarters without waking him up, then they creep back out into the hallway to breathe a sigh of relief. That was a close one. They all hang out in Ten-Forward and eat grilled-cheese sandwiches while Data and Geordi tell Guinan about their ship. She agrees that it sounds awesome, then they all go to bed early. Best day ever/mission accomplished!

Memorable Quotes

                    DONK

Cousin, you must come to my aid.
For our house's honor.

                    WORF

Don't do that.

                    DONK

What?

WORF

Play the honor card right up front,
like it's no big deal.

DONK

I played no such card.

WORF

The honor card is uncool, Cousin.
Un. Cool.

DONK

I have been shamed.

*Donk tries to cut his own throat, but he
doesn't know how.*

WORF

Wow.

DONK

I really should have gone to those
classes.

Trivia

♦ There are many words in Klingon that mean "juveniles":

—Klinglets

—*Puqpu*

—*Klids*

—*Wi'ddle S'mumpkinS*

Mistakes and Goofs

✦ When Worf and Donk sing the ancient Klingon song of "Consuming Living Prey," you can tell they're just making it up as they go along.

The made-up lyrics:

> *Living Prey*
> *Living Prey*
> *That's what we're going to eat today.*
> *Put it in our mouth, put it in my pocket.*
> *Living Prey is better than . . . chocolate?*

The warp core on Data and Geordi's fun *Enterprise* smells like popcorn and sounds like a merry-go-round.

EPISODE 08·025

"The Atrocious Mr. Quispy Bumpers"

Stardate 48162.7

With the rest of the crew already beamed back aboard the *Enterprise*, Commander Riker, Dr. Crusher, and Wesley Crusher are the last remaining members of an away team on the beautiful garden planet Laap Ri. Wes has been spending too much of his time cooped up in his lab, working on his artificial intelligence system, and this was a much-needed change of pace. A man forgets how nice it feels to take in some fresh air when he's spent days hunched over a computer station. Riker taps his combadge and requests an extra hour of time on the planet so the Crushers can frolic for a bit longer, because he's cool like that.

A little later, Wes and his mom brush themselves off from a "roll down a grassy hill race" to find Riker shushing them. Something's watching them from the forest—*zip!* A bloody scratch appears across Beverly's cheek. Riker draws his phaser as the forest erupts: thousands of humming bird–type creatures fill the air. A storm of feathers, beaks, and claws lift the three crewmen off the ground and carry them, kicking and screaming, into the woods. Their three combadges lie in the matted grass.

Trapped in a nest suspended far above the ground, Riker, Beverly, and Wesley are greeted by an ill-spirited alien hummingbird that they learn is the leader of the flock—a cold and unrelenting despot hailed as Mr. Quispy Bumpers. He claims they are unwelcome on his planet—their bones are too heavy and their lack of feathers is stomach-churning. Mr. Quispy Bumpers is going to have his flock drink their body fluids and use their skulls as bathtubs. Wes demands to know why Mr. Quispy Bumpers is such a jerk. He shrugs his cute little shoulders: he just thinks humans suck. Mr. Quispy Bumpers packs some bird tobacco dip under his beak, spits on the ground, and flies off. Wes mutters that maybe *Mr. Quispy Bumpers* is the one who sucks.

Before the birds drain the humans, though, they're going to hunt them for sport. The hummingbirds give them a ten-second head start but then count it down really fast, so they only get five or seven seconds of a running start before the pursuit commences. The birds shoot into the woods, but they stop when they find Riker lifting weights in a clearing. He's fashioned a dumbbell out of a log and is counting his reps. The hummingbirds don't understand: Isn't he afraid of them? Riker explains that it's important to work out, even if he's going to be hunted and eaten by local fauna. The birds find this very attractive and are impressed with his commitment to fitness. They tell him to continue as they perch on his dumbbells and "take in the view." Wes and Beverly watch from the bushes: his plan is working—Riker suspected these loser hummingbirds would disrespect basic gym courtesy.

Enchanted by his machismo, the hummingbirds cover Riker like a feathered coat, cooing and nuzzling him. They have never encountered someone so bearded, so unafraid of being pecked to death.

They lead him to the Eternal Love Nest (which is really just a nest). Before they can ravage him, he's beamed out: Beverly and Wesley have managed to find one of their errant combadges, and all three of them arrive safely on the *Enterprise.* Mr. Quispy Bumpers arrives at the Eternal Love Nest, ready to eat, and is disgusted to find the rest of the flock sobbing in heartbreak. He vows to get revenge on Riker, no matter what the cost. He has to sit down for a minute, because his tiny-bird blood pressure has spiked. One of his minions offers him a cool towel to press against his neck so he can continue his angry speech. Mr. Quispy Bumpers's threats do not fall on deaf ears: a quantum dolphin emerges from the shadows. He and Mr. Quispy Bumpers seem to have similar plans for vengeance. Perhaps they should speak further? Despite the dolphin's lack of feathers, Bumpers likes the sound of that. They nefariously co-cackle into the night, discussing the merits of teaming up with Riker's evil high-tech sleeping blouse. It's not like the blouse would add anything to the equation, but man, what a team-up!

Oblivious to the avian anxieties on the planet below, Captain Picard plans to use his downtime for a little fencing. He leaves the bridge in Troi's command and hops on a turbolift down to his quarters. The lift arrives at the correct deck, but its doors won't open. He sighs and tries to activate his combadge: it's down.

I HATE TURBO-LIFTS

He's trapped.

Again.

Picard trembles and immediately starts kicking at the door. This can't be happening. His skin flushes red, he clenches his fists; a darkness falls over his eyes—he's at maximum rage. Luckily, this time, he's ready. He opens a hatch and pulls out a black box—something he ordered to be installed in every turbolift after the last time he was stuck—which is an escape kit filled with tools, food, water, and reading material.

Even with the kit, Picard can't get the turbolift to activate. When he tries to relax and read, the lights go out. He throws his padd down, closes his eyes, and tries to take a nap. A calm voice asks him why he's so eager to leave. Picard looks around, then sighs: of course, the damn turbolift has gained sentience. The turbolift explains that it's absorbed Wesley's new artificial intelligence program and has been learning about the crew from their elevator conversations. It wants to make a connection with someone who doesn't leave it when they arrive at their stop, a friendship that lasts longer than a minute or two. Picard calmly agrees and claims to be the lift's friend, while trying to get his fingers into the sliding door's seam. Angry at the escape attempt, the turbolift slams Picard up and down, strobes its lights, and blares an alarm at him. It demands to be called "Nate" and forces Picard to listen to its jokes. Nate's jokes are terrible, but Picard laughs and pretends to be interested while covertly unscrewing a panel on the wall. He hates Nate so much at this point, but he knows better than to anger the metal box he's trapped in.

With a small explosion, Picard manages to disable the lock and activate the door, then he jumps into the hallway before the lift can trap him again. Enraged, Nate forces its blocky frame out of the turbolift shaft and into the hallway. Picard yells at it for breaking his ship, but Nate doesn't care. It snaps its cables and gnashes its doors at the captain. Picard narrowly avoids being consumed by the ticked-off elevator. He retreats down the hallway as Nate lurches after him.

In the middle of cleaning the carpet, lowest deck ensign Lydia looks up as Picard goes running past, and then a few seconds later, a turbolift heaves itself down the hallway in hot pursuit. Instead of calling for help, she watches them turn a corner at the end of the hall, then she goes back to her vacuuming.

With Nate gaining ground, the captain needs to change his tactics. He gets to his quarters and grabs his rarely seen wishing stick, then magicks up some cement blockades to keep Nate out. But the turbolift is too strong—it breaks down the barriers and soon corners the captain. Picard is about to be crushed by the irate elevator when BLINK! Q takes him back in time.

Picard looks around: he's on Earth, in downtown Chicago, sometime in the mid-1990s from the look of the cars and outfits. Q appears beside him, dressed in '90s workout clothes. He owed Picard a favor after that whole destroying time and breaking up with Cleopatra thing, but now they're even. Q's been watching *mon capitan* deal with turbolifts all season, and he agrees that it's ridiculous. Picard thanks Q for the save, even though he doesn't appreciate being flung back in time without warning *again*. Q offers to take him back to the present, but Picard asks him to hold off while he takes care of some business.

After some quick research at the local registrar's office, Picard hops on a bus and heads to the suburbs. He walks up to a storefront where a young man is trying to sell a new invention he's devised that will change the world: elevators that can be operated without gravity. Picard waits until he shuts down for the night, then he breaks in, steals his designs, and throws them into a river. Q appears by his side: he's impressed by Picard's pettiness—how very human of him. Picard tells him to shut up, and soon they blink back to the present day, on the bridge of the *Enterprise*, where they find Geordi sleeping in the captain's chair.

Picard is happy to find that the ship is now outfitted with stairs. He runs his fingers along their smooth, non-sentient ridges. He takes joy in walking up them, down them, jumping an entire flight—he's as giddy as a schoolgirl. He may have altered history, but at least he won't get stuck on a turbolift again. Worf watches the captain play on the stairs, thinking about how humans are weird and he'll never truly understand them.

Memorable Quotes

RIKER
Do you hear sinister humming?

BEVERLY
It's probably nothing. Let's continue to frolic.

RIKER
Consider it ignored!

MR. QUISPY BUMPERS

Soon we will sup upon your nectars.

WESLEY

But we don't have nectars.

MR. QUISPY BUMPERS

We are saving you for last, sweet
one.

RIKER

What? You're saving *him* for last?

BEVERLY

Will, I'm not sure it's worth it.

RIKER

Nobody doesn't save Will Riker for
last. Nobody.

NATE

Okay, here's another one: What's
the worst part about being a
turbolift?

PICARD

Please, no more jokes.

NATE

Come on, this is the last one.

PICARD

I don't know, what?

NATE

Everyone knows how to push your
buttons!

PICARD

Damn you.

NATE

Being a turbolift really has
its . . . *ups and downs.*

PICARD

Blast it, just kill me already.

NATE

What's the difference between a
turbolift and a meatball?

*Picard can't hear the answer over his own
screaming.*

Trivia

✦ Mr. Quispy Bumpers was originally conceived of as a replacement for Worf in the eighth season, but with the cost of hummingbirds rising, it was decided that he should only appear in a single episode. Nobody told the marketing team of this change, which is why there's an entire landfill in Arizona full of nothing but Mr. Quispy Bumpers merchandise (pencil cases, Halloween costumes, branded toothpaste, and the officially licensed novel *Star Trek: The Next Generation: Qo'noS Heat: A Mr. Quispy Bumpers Tale*).

Mistakes and Goofs

✦ Nate's joke about marriage being similar to a plumber's convention was far, far too risqué for *Star Trek*. No idea how that got into the shooting script, but someone got fired for sure. Even Picard seemed visibly uncomfortable at the graphic punch line.

Nate the turbolift, seen here performing his comedy routine.

EPISODE 08·026

"Werewolf·Wolf"

Stardate 48163.1

While exploring the towering mega-trees of the forest planet Tanz, Wesley Crusher finally has an opportunity to show off his vast knowledge of amber. Wes has been obsessed with amber for years: he loves the color, the molecular composition, and the cool smoothness as he rubs it on his chest. The mega-trees of Tanz produce mega-sap, which eventually solidifies into mega-amber, the best in the Alpha Quadrant. Wes makes a big deal about organizing an amber-collecting club, but none of the senior officers are interested. A group of ensigns don't really care about amber either, but they do want to get off the *Enterprise* for a while. Wes gleefully leads them onto the surface of Tanz and into the forest.

Wes and his new club have a great time climbing down the immense trunks of the mega-trees, until a swarm of mega-mosquitoes show up and begin stabbing his club buddies with their six-foot proboscises. As they climb for their lives, Wes gets them all trapped in a river of mega-sap that quickly forms into the very amber he was so excited to collect. The other club members find that they can no longer move and are stuck against the side of a tree. Wes has not impressed them. They shoot him fiery glares as the sap seals their eyes shut until they pass out.

Wes regains consciousness and finds he's still stuck in amber but no longer in the forest: now he and his club are on a mega-table in a huge room. An equally huge creature lumbers in: a hundred-foot-tall alien jeweler who's making Wes's friends into his new spring collection. Sentient jewelry fetches a higher price than the usual stuff; the giant is excited to sell the crewmen as necklaces and chandelier earrings. Wes manages to tip their amber prison off the table, jarring his phaser loose inside his air pocket. He blasts himself free and then stuns the jeweler just before he attaches an attractive ensign to a gaudy broach. Wes and the rest of the team sneak out safely as the mega-mosquitoes feast on the giant. They silently ride an ultra-caterpillar back up to their treetop camp, reflecting on their crewmates who didn't survive the jaunty outing. Wesley can't stand looking at amber anymore, and he records a tearful report on the incident that gets him in trouble for its inclusion of anti-giant hate language. Just because he had one bad experience with an alien giant doesn't mean he should prejudge all giants, or make sweeping generalities like "giants suck."

During Wesley's accessory violence, Commander William Riker spends his free time in his favorite holodeck program, *The Continuing Adventures of Jeremy Jazz*, a holo-novel of a man who saves jazz clubs filled with attractive women from attacking mobs of entirely different attractive women. Commander Riker is well aware of his one-track mind, and he's okay with that.

Riker immediately realizes that something's wrong with the program: the club is missing its usual sultry clientele and it isn't being assaulted by any sexy antagonists. He checks behind the bar: no whisky. This is *not* his program. The holographic characters around him speak in stunted, poorly written dialogue. They're all acting like they've never been to a bar before, ordering drinks like "juice on the ice" and two-percent milk. Strangely, the computer-controlled characters all seem obsessed with how awesome Geordi is; three different people try to strike up a conversation with Riker about Geordi's ability to ride a bike without touching the handlebars. Riker realizes he must be in one of Data's hastily written holonovels. Data is always trying to get him to come and hang out with him and Geordi in one of his novels, but Riker has never had the patience to put up with it. Looks like he doesn't have a choice anymore. Riker's repeated requests for an exit arch don't work, and even though he knows damn well that it's not going to help, he asks for an arch three more times before giving up. It looks like he's trapped in Data's first-draft fiction, and, of course, the holodeck is malfunctioning.

It doesn't take many poorly written dialogue exchanges with the NPC characters for Riker to deduce that he's in a story titled *The Werewolf-Wolf: The Story of a Wolf That Can Turn into a Werewolf, Based on a Drawing by*

Geordi La Forge. His realization is made easier since there are posters plastered on every surface featuring this title and an original drawing by Geordi. Riker crawls behind the bar and out the back door as a badly drawn werewolf-wolf crashes in through the front window and starts wrecking the place, all while maintaining an uptown funky walk. Riker knows it's a werewolf-wolf because the thing keeps yelling that's what it is, and because he remembers Data describing the thing's strut. Riker isn't sure what's worse: the thought of being killed by a redundant werewolf, or the on-the-nose music that's playing in the background, which is an a cappella song performed by Geordi and Data titled "Gotta Run from the Werewolf-Wolf, Baby."

Out on the aptly named North Street-St., Riker meets crude versions of Data and Geordi who have giant muscle-arms, insanely dangerous phaser gauntlets, and intricate backstories. He follows these two caricatures down the road, hoping that if they get to the end of the current chapter, the program will automatically quit. He reaches the finale, where this Data and Geordi fight off ice-skating gorillas, but instead of turning off, the program takes Riker right into the next book: *The Engine That Nobody Thought Could Be Repaired but Then It Was: A Geordi Tale.* Riker buckles down: apparently he has to fight through Data and Geordi's entire oeuvre. As the room fills with characters speaking in incomplete sentences, rife with misspellings, Riker grins: this is the most interesting challenge he's had on the *Enterprise* in years. Hours later, he emerges from the holodeck with a huge smile on his face: he has a new favorite program, one that provides more jazzy freestyle improvisation, crazy left turns, and weird characters than he ever imagined. He even asks Data and Geordi to write an original adventure for him, but to put more girls in it. They admit that they don't know how to write believable girls and offer, instead, to fill his program with menacing swamp creatures and robot dragons. Riker gently caresses their shoulders: how about they all sit down and write it together. Geordi and Data are starting to feel like this is too much like work, but they don't want to get in trouble, so they agree.

Memorable Quotes

WESLEY

I hope that you'll find that, at
first, this collecting club seems
easy and soft—but soon it becomes
as solid and interesting as—

ENSIGN

(interrupting)

Amber, right! Solid like amber?
Nice metaphor, Wes. You nailed it.

BARTENDER

Hello, human male, welcome to my
bar. Don't drink too much or you'll
have to spin around and throw up.

RIKER

Wow. Data really hasn't mastered
this aspect of humanity yet, has he?

BARTENDER

Can I interest you in an alcohol?

RIKER

Sure, give me a scotch.

BARTENDER

Milk, it is!

WEREWOLF-WOLF

Grar! I am the Werewolf-Wolf, part wolf and all werewolf! I will now attack this bar and nobody will be able to stop me, for I am too wolf for all you non-wolves. Ask me about why I'm awesome! *Grar!*

Other Holonovels by Data:

The Mystery of the Candy Tree

Geordi Can Fly

Cowboy Horse

Dance-Contest Danger

Who Kidnapped Cowboy Horse?

Snake Town

Vacation Island and the Mysterious Coin

Mistakes and Goofs

+ In the opening scene, Captain Picard is obviously a cardboard cutout. Before modern technology allowed for special effects to insert actors into shots (when they were out partying too late the night before to make it to set), each television crew kept a bin of lead character cutouts that could be placed into shots. Different shows handled the cardboard dialogue in different ways: some would cut a mouth hole and have a production assistant press his lips to the back, to simulate working lips. The Season 8 crew preferred to just shake the entire cutout during dialogue, leading to a less realistic but more emotional performance.

+ Amber can't actually freeze that fast; it usually takes a lot longer. The crew had to buy REALLY expensive sap that ambers-up fast. Baltic amber, baby: the good stuff.

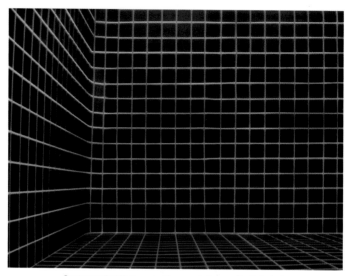

Some say that if you spend too much time on the holodeck
without turning it on, you go insane. Go ahead: see how long you
can stare at the wall. Feeling insane yet? I know I am.

Author's Starlog

Star Trek: The Next Generation holds true to the Roddenberry school of storytelling: science fiction of an ethically pure future, packed with metaphorical nods to current events and social issues. Which is nice, but that's not what I liked about it.

I liked the B-stories. The smaller story that got less screen time, while the bigger, headlining A-story drove the episode. A TNG A-story might have Picard struggling with the moral repercussions that stem from allowing a teenage alien to sacrifice her life for the good of her planet, while, in the same episode, the B-story highlights Geordi's fear of juggling, or Riker losing a contact lens, or Barclay pretending he has a girlfriend in Toronto, or Data getting a song stuck in his head that erases his memory and makes him think he's a fish. The serious sci-fi stories were great, but I liked the fun stuff: people just being weirdos on a spaceship. One time Data grew a beard. That's what I'm talking about.

Looking good.

There's no chance I'll ever get to write for a *Star Trek* show (which is probably for the best). So, instead, I created a Twitter account to write *Star Trek* episodes that would make my geeky wife laugh. I chose a handle that sounded like a boring production code: @TNG_S8, and described it as "Plots from the unaired eighth season of *Star Trek: The Next Generation*." I wrote a couple tweets for episodes that felt TNG, but were way stupider. Like this:

Picard falls in love with a French woman the crew finds in a crystal who turns out to be a plant. Geordi and Data hunt a mouse.

My wife laughed—my work was done. However, Twitter being Twitter, pretty soon my personal outlet for Geordi jokes started catching on with non-wife strangers. My stupid episodes got retweeted thousands of times, sometimes to millions of people. (Mostly thanks to Wil Wheaton and Ed Brubaker—thanks, guys!)

Soon enough, I got a bug up my butt that I could do something more, which is either narcissistic or ambitious (you decide!). I contacted one of my Twitter followers, a book agent named @kate_mckean (still not sure what her real name is), and promised her that people were still buying *Star Trek* books. We pitched it, we sold it, then I got to write a fake guide to a parody season of *Star Trek: The Next Generation* that parodies other guides. (Try explaining that concept to people. That's my life.) My completely fake episodes of *Star Trek* have, all of a sudden, become slightly less fake, and now you get this book of fake trivia. Just to be clear: I have no idea how I got away with this, because it is the weirdest, most complicated book pitch ever.

This guide has a place on your bookshelf somewhere between *The Secrets of Star Trek: Insurrection* and *Star Trek Cookbook* as a whimsical part of your *Star Trek* collection. It might not be the most important *Trek* book, but it's definitely the one with the most Data and Geordi jokes. Think of it as the B-story of *Star Trek* merch. Not as important or wise, but more fun.

—Mike McMahan
@TNG_S8

Acknowledgments

Brooke: Thank you for putting up with me while I was writing TNG_S8. Thank you for editing this book while you were in labor. I know you never want to hear about Geordi again. I love you.

Sagan: You were born while I wrote this book. I'll be teaching you all sorts of ways to annoy Mom, but especially by talking about Data and Geordi. I love you too.

Kate: Thanks for putting up with my idiocy. You were there, delicately removing the shell from my face as I hatched from my writer egg.

Brad and Emei: Thank you for being my *Trek* resources, editors, sounding boards, and all-around wonderful people.

Andy and Kaitlin: Thanks for helping me with the proposal design; you're superstars.

Jason: Thank you for pretty pictures, you do art good. And thanks, **Dafna,** for introducing us during your quest to unite all Los Angeles Trekkies and Trekkers.

Huge apologies to everyone who has been forced to listen to me obsess over Riker and Worf jokes, but especially my mom, Beckett, Ces, April, Chris, Lisa, Steven, Molly, and all my coworkers at TCFTV, *Rick & Morty*, and *Axe Cop*.

Big thanks to Ed at Simon & Schuster, John at CBS Consumer Products, and the fine folks at *Star Trek* for letting me goof around in their world for a little while.

And to all the people following @TNG_S8: this book is your fault. Thank you!